An **Ecstasy Romance**™

HIS REFLEXES WERE AS SWIFT
AS HER OWN. . . .

She didn't get a chance for a second blow. He grabbed her wrists and immobilized them behind her back with almost contemptuous strength.

Raine ceased her writhing abruptly when she realized that he was enjoying, responding to, the stimulation of her captive body as it strained to free itself. . . .

"Fight me some more, little wildcat," he whispered huskily into her ear as she stood rigidly in the unbreakable enclosure of his arms. "Let's melt that ice you try to chill me with. There's fire inside you. I want to warm myself in your flames. . . ."

CANDLELIGHT ECSTASY ROMANCES™

COME LOVE,
CALL MY NAME

Anne N. Reisser

A CANDLELIGHT ECSTASY ROMANCE™

Published by
Dell Publishing Co., Inc.
1 Dag Hammarskjold Plaza
New York, New York 10017

Dell ® TM 681510, Dell Publishing Co., Inc.

Candlelight Ecstasy Romance™ is a trademark of
Dell Publishing Co., Inc., New York, New York.

ISBN: 0-440-11321-0

Printed in the United States of America

First printing—August 1982

Dear Reader:

In response to your continued enthusiasm for Candlelight Ecstasy Romances™, we are increasing the number of new titles from four to six per month.

We are delighted to present sensuous novels set in America, depicting modern American men and women as they confront the provocative problems of modern relationships.

Throughout the history of the Candlelight line, Dell has tried to maintain a high standard of excellence, to give you the finest in reading enjoyment. That is now and will remain our most ardent ambition.

Anne Gisonny
Editor
Candlelight Romances

CHAPTER I

It was instinct . . . and superb timing and muscular coordination . . . with no tinge of conscious heroics. When she saw the speeding car bearing down on the older woman who stood in its destructive path, frozen by a mind-blinding panic, Raine reacted automatically. Her knapsack and precious portfolio fell behind her as she sprinted toward the petrified woman. With split-second timing, but no gentleness, she got them both back from the imminent reality of a gory death beneath the hot, screeching tires of the juggernaut car.

The grinding scream of brakes tore through the background hum of the ceaseless bustle of cars and buses, the sharp sound splitting the fabric of normal activity beyond easy repair. The squealing acceleration of the tires as the car wove its deadly path through its tamer metal kin might have been a hunting cry, proclaiming that, having been thwarted from claiming its intended prey, the car was seeking other, less agile, game.

The babbling chorus from the inevitable crowd rose to cover the fading sound of the car's erratic and deadly progress away from the scene of the near tragedy. "Driving like a maniac . . ." "Must have been high on something!" "Never saw anyone move so fast in my life. If it hadn't been for the girl . . ." "Somebody call a cop!" "If it hadn't been for the girl, he'd have run the old lady down like a streetside cat."

Then, from the distance, came the grinding sound of a collision followed by the anxious hush that denotes shock and arrested motion at the scene of a disaster in the seconds before life and motion flow onward to their grim conclusion. The useless babble rose again shrilly, a repetitive chorus of "Somebody call a cop . . ."

Raine lifted her head wearily, looking up from the sprawled body of the woman she had thrown and rolled to rough safety. "I rather think there'll be several policemen in the vicinity very soon." She answered one of the more vocal members of the gaping throng with a touch of asperity. No one seemed disposed to accomplish anything constructive, but Raine had often found that to be the case. There are those who do and those who talk. . . .

Raine assisted the ashen-faced woman to her feet and guided her to a low wall nearby. She sat beside her, half-supporting the trembling body with her own bruised and dusty frame. She murmured soothing sounds to the sobbing woman who was repeating, in the trembling accents of shock, "I didn't see him. I didn't see him and then it was too late. I couldn't move. I couldn't move."

"Sssh. It's all right now. You're safe now. Nothing happened. You're safe," Raine crooned over and over, much as she had crooned to countless frightened animals in her childhood. Raine had an abiding weakness for the lame dog, and her family had long since resigned itself to that ineradicable, and at times, highly inconvenient, trait of her strongly developed character.

Her calming ministrations began to have predictable effects and the shaken woman shuddered a final time and sighed deeply. The sorrowing wail of fast approaching ambulances indicated that, for others in the path of the deadly vehicle, there had been no Raine to risk and reclaim life from certain death.

For reasons of her own, Raine had no desire to have the incident come under official scrutiny, but she couldn't leave the job half-done. The woman she had saved was in no condition to reach her intended destination alone, wherever and whatever that had been. Well, her own plans had a certain amount of flexibility, and she really had no choice. She detested half-done jobs!

"I don't know how to thank you . . ." the older woman began, but Raine shushed her firmly.

"I just happened to be in the right place, but now I think that it'd be best if we got you home where you can rest a bit, and perhaps see your family doctor."

"No! No more doctors!" There was an almost hysterical emphasis in the refusal. "Doctors can't help me anymore," the woman continued bitterly, her hands beginning to twist and entwine in her lap.

Raine could sense the sharply rising agitation and she spoke hastily to stem the incipient relapse into hysteria. "Where do you live? I'll go with you to your home. You don't have to see a doctor if you'd rather not." The soothing cadences worked their calming magic once more and this time Raine was able to extract a name and destination from her companion.

Mary Hunter was, like Raine, a visitor to the city and, like Raine, she had planned to leave the next day, but their purposes in coming to San Francisco could not have been more at variance. Raine had come to the city as the last lap in a journey that was to bring her back to life. Mary Hunter had come to San Francisco to receive a sentence of death.

Raine gathered her scattered belongings and, to the bemusement of the watching crowd, gestured imperiously at a cruising cab. It pulled over to the curb obediently, causing many of the men watching to wonder why *their* frantic wavings and whistlings had never accomplished what her simple flick of the wrist had wrought. Raine could have told them that she had perfected the art of cab-summoning in London and that it consisted of a combination of arrogant certainty that the cab would respond, the bait of having a shapely figure (which was currently well displayed by her clean but faded jeans and a figure-caressing knit shirt), and some indefinable *je ne sais quoi* which was almost a psychic force. She desired a cab . . . and one came. She also had an uncanny knack for finding the last parking space in the lot or for having a car vacate one just where and when she needed it.

For the first time in a long time Raine was actively grateful for her "gift." She bundled her recently and dramatically acquired charge into the idling cab and gave the driver the name of the hotel as supplied by her companion. With a calm authority in no way diminished by her exceedingly casual style of dress

12

and her disheveled appearance, Raine shepherded Mary Hunter into her luxurious hotel, obtained the suite key, and installed her in the comfortable rooms with maximum speed and minimum fuss. A brisk order to room service brought hot sweet tea for Mary and a pot of coffee for Raine.

Raine didn't allow time for shock to develop. On her orders Mary downed the hot tea and was assisted into a warming and relaxing tub, and only after she was clean, cosseted, and tucked firmly into the comfortable bed did Raine allow her to express finally the thanks for the gift of her life, to loose the words which had been waiting impatiently for release ever since Raine had helped her to rise from the hard ground.

"You *must* allow me to tell you how grateful I am to you, my dear," Mary insisted. "You risked your own life to save mine and I must be allowed to recognize that fact. I have just recently realized how precious the days of my life are to me." A shadow crossed her face, but she met Raine's eyes bravely.

All of Raine's senses trilled alert. Faces were her business and this face was marked with a knowledge not accepted by many—the resigned acceptance of mortality. Raine had seen such realization before in the faces of the very old and the very ill, but at first glance Mary Hunter was neither.

"Would you like to talk about it?" Raine questioned quietly.

The older woman looked at her sharply, measuring the truth and compassion that burned like a gentle blue fire in Raine's eyes. "You know!" she stated flatly. "*How* do you know?"

"I have seen Death," Raine answered simply. "It comes in many guises, but to those who have foreknowledge and a measure of acceptance there is a certain look . . ." Both shapely hands gestured with an encompassing, wordless motion.

"Who are you?"

"My name is Raine Fisher," Raine introduced herself.

"No, not just your name," the older woman said impatiently. "*Who* are you, that so young you can recognize us? Are you one of us?"

"No, not in the way you mean it," Raine answered. "Like all who live, I do so under the long sentence of eventual physical dissolution, but I haven't received my personal notice." She hesitated and then said, "My full name is Raine *Talbot* Fisher."

"Talbot?" The emphasis on the name had been unmistakable, but it took a moment for Mary Hunter to make the connection. To help her, Raine unstrapped her portfolio and carefully withdrew several sheets of stiff white paper. She removed the protective tissue interleaves. One by one she handed the squares of paper to the other woman.

"Talbot." Now there was recognition, even if it was tinged with disbelief. On each piece of paper was a face, and in each face there was an unmistakable, sometimes agonizing individuality, a portrait of a human at crisis point. Young faces, old faces: there was no commonality of age, but each bore the marks of life. There were no smooth, self-satisfied faces. The faces Raine had captured were gaunt with a hunger of the spirit, if not of the flesh.

"You can't be that Talbot," Mary floundered. The woman who sat in a chair by her bed was young, in her mid-twenties. Her face was smooth, with only a few raying sun lines at the corners of her deep blue eyes. Her mouth was sweet and generous and her sun-streaked golden hair was casually but stylishly cut. She might have been any young suburban woman but for the clarity of her gaze. Those eyes saw through the mask of face to the spirit beneath, and the slender hands that now rested so quietly in her lap had the power to translate that sharp vision into deft lines of portraits and scenes. She painted and drew the human condition: good, evil, sad, funny . . . the spectrum of life.

"How . . . how can you see so deeply?" The older woman faltered, unable to reconcile the youth and femininity of Raine with the powerful vision and incisive clarity of a Talbot portrait or scene.

Raine hesitated. The price she had paid for the maturity that enabled her to paint as she did had been a high one, and one she had never discussed with anyone. Even her family had never fully understood, though they had tried. Only Johnny, darling, beloved Johnny who had been part of the price, could have understood fully.

But this woman had asked, and because she was who and what she was, because Raine had just given Mary Hunter the gift of the remaining days of her life, Raine would try to help her understand what had been so painfully learned.

"I married Johnny Fisher when I was eighteen," Raine said quietly. "He was twenty and I'd known him all my life. We were always a pair: Johnny-and-

15

Raine, said like one word. My parents and his had wanted us to wait to get married, for me to go to college and for him to finish his studies. There was no opposition to our marriage, you understand. They just thought that there was plenty of time for us."

Her face was still while her eyes looked back into time, and there was the tight shadow of an old, deep pain over her skin. "We had so little time. A month before we married the doctors diagnosed a rare and fatal blood disorder. They gave Johnny a year or two at most. We had three years." Her eyes were dark with memory.

Then, with an obvious effort, Raine returned to the present and the sympathetic eyes of the woman who watched her quietly. "After Johnny died, I cut myself off from life. He had prepared himself for death and he went gallantly, but I hadn't done so well. I was not prepared for life without him. He'd always been there for me, and without him the world was empty and useless. There was nothing of value left to me. I was a coward, you see. Johnny was brave. He took life on its own terms and came up a winner, but I ran away. If the game wasn't run by *my* rules, I wouldn't play."

"My dear, please don't. It isn't necessary." Mary tried to stem the painful revelations. Raine's face was still expressionless, but her eyes held the refreshed memories of the torment of that time.

"I must," Raine said simply. "I've never tried to put this into words before, and for your sake and mine also, I'll finish what I started. Call it a last step back to life." She resumed her narrative. "For six months I opted out of life. I don't mean I turned to

16

drugs or alcohol, I just locked myself away inside my mind. I went through the motions. I ate, I slept, I talked, but nothing and no one really touched or got through to me. I know now that my family and Johnny's family were suffering too, but he had been *mine,* of my flesh, and I hugged my pain because in a twisted way it was the only link I had left. It is so hard to be the one left behind." Raine sighed.

Mary sat quietly, her eyes never leaving Raine's face. She might have been the ensorcelled victim of the Ancient Mariner, wound in a web of words which must spin to their conclusion before the pattern of the tale allowed release for the helpless victim.

Raine continued. "Then, six months after Johnny's death, his mother came to see me. She sat me down and she put it to me plainly. Johnny was dead. Nothing could change that. I had to accept that fact and start to get on with my life again. She said something to me that I'll carry as a talisman for the rest of my life. She said: 'Love should strengthen, Raine, not weaken. Johnny's love for you was the finest thing in his life. It gave him the courage to live and then, when the time came, it gave him the courage to die. Let his love for you give you the courage to live without him.' That was the first step back to life for me."

"It's been a long road back." Raine's low voice was husky. "I'd always painted, and Johnny had always encouraged me, so I decided to see what I could really do. I wanted . . . needed . . . to be on my own. Five years ago I began a nomad's life, traveling and painting. I haven't been home except for short

17

visits, to leave my completed works and to assure my parents and Johnny's that I'm finding my way back, slowly but steadily. I've roved the world and I've met people. I've seen them live and I've seen them die, some gallantly, like my Johnny, and some with a wail and a whimper. I've seen things that have sickened me and things which have uplifted me and through it all I've painted. I've looked for answers in faces and sometimes I've found them. All of life is a quest for answers, but when you've found one answer, there's always another question. If you quit looking, you die, and I don't mean die physically. A refusal to live to the fullest possible extent is to be dead and soul-stunted. Life is never fair, but it's the most exciting play in town."

"Even when the play is only a limited engagement?" Mary couldn't keep the bitterness from spilling into her voice.

"None of us has any guarantees from one breath to the next, Mary," Raine said evenly. "It's the quality, the intensity of the time that gives it meaning, not its duration. If you look back over the length of your life, are you satisfied with its quality? Have you done the important things; have you given and received love? If not, then you have an opportunity given to very few of us: to enhance the quality of your life, knowing the value of the time you have left. Spend your remaining minutes and hours wisely and you'll realize that they'll be worth more than all that has gone before, because now you truly value them."

Raine's blunt pronouncement sent a wave of color flushing over the pale skin of the reclining woman. Her stunning sentence of death had been shrouded in muffling platitudes and cushioned by half-hopes, but Raine had cut through to the bone. She, Mary Hunter, was going to die. Raine was challenging her to *live* until she died!

Raine saw Mary flinch at the brutal frankness of her words, but she didn't try to soften them. They were linked because of Raine's impulsive action, and Raine was now constrained by the implicit truth contained in the old Chinese proverb that to save a life was to become responsible for it. She had given Mary Hunter additional days and she felt obligated to help the woman utilize them to her fullest capacity.

The flush had faded and Raine noticed that now Mary's color could charitably be called wan. She leaned forward and patted the hand lying limply on the coverlet. "I think that this is enough for now. You've had a bad experience and I prescribe the best medicine . . . a nap. We'll talk later."

Mary grabbed at her hand as though it represented a lifeline she couldn't relinquish. "You won't go while I sleep?" she gasped desperately. "You won't leave me? Please?"

"No, Mary. I won't leave you yet. We'll talk more when you've rested. I promise." Raine gently reassured the anxious woman.

While Mary slept, Raine showered and changed into clean clothes. For five years she had traveled, experiencing living conditions varying from the most primitive to the most comfortable. She had slept in mud huts, under star-icy skies, and in the houses of the rich and the poor. She had learned to be infinitely adaptable about her personal surroundings, but she'd

19

never lost her appreciation for a nice hot shower! She scrubbed vigorously at her hair, working the rich shampoo down to her scalp, wincing once when she hit a tender spot where her skull had contacted the hard street during that frantic roll and scramble away from the merciless wheels of the killer car. She'd also acquired several scrapes and bruises on other parts of her body, but they were minor, of little consequence.

The long-term consequences of her impulsive rescue wouldn't be physical, but they would be nonetheless far-reaching. At least she had been able to avoid publicity of any sort! Raine shunned any and all forms of limelight. Her one-man shows in the art galleries hung and sold out without her presence. Many people weren't sure whether "Talbot" was male or female and the owner of the gallery through which her work was funneled knew that it was worth his life to even hint anything about the identity of his reclusive client.

The Talbots and the Fishers were low-profile old-money families with strongly developed social consciences unusual for their social strata and financial ratings. The Talbots were bankers; the Fishers concentrated on transportation and energy. The families were linked in friendship, business, and by marriage. Raine and Johnny had not been the first marriage between the families; they themselves had been second cousins through their respective mother's sides, and the clans were far-flung and intertwined.

Even though the families were business-oriented, the occasional artistic cuckoo in the family nest was encouraged and pridefully acknowledged. Raine had been protected and cherished throughout her early life, but neither money nor family connections had been able to save Johnny!

After she had dressed in clean jeans and another knit shirt, Raine reentered the darkened bedroom where Mary Hunter lay peacefully asleep. Raine checked her pulse and breathing cautiously. Mary stirred slightly but sank easily back into deep slumber when Raine released her wrist. Raine passed through the bedroom to the living room where she placed a long distance phone call charged to her personal credit card. Her parents had been anticipating her arrival on a transcontinental flight tomorrow afternoon, but Raine knew that she wouldn't be able to leave Mary yet.

Her mother was disappointed but resigned. She knew her daughter well and knew that Raine would be unable to resist the special appeal inherent in Mary Hunter's circumstances. Raine had never been a person who was particularly bound by schedules and the past five years had increased, rather than diminished, her tendency to measure all time by activities, rather than by dividing it into minutes, days, and months. When she decided that her self-imposed job of helping Mary Hunter was completed to the best of her ability, Raine would come home. How long would she stay this time? Who knew?

Since Johnny's death Raine had wandered the world, returning periodically to renew ties with her family, but she had shown no desire to ever again be fettered within a fixed abode. Had it not been for the maturity and compassion easily discernible in her paintings, those who loved her would have worried about her more than they did. They worried about her physical safety, and rightly so, but not about her mental health. Raine was no longer escaping from life. She had gone out to meet it head on.

Raine amused herself by flipping through the TV channels, noting that neither the quality nor the content of the programs available had improved markedly since her last visit to the States. She tuned into a classical station on the FM radio and settled down to read a battered paperback edition of *The Dancing Wu Li Masters.*

Late in the afternoon she heard Mary stirring in the bedroom. She marked her place, returned the volume to the depths of her knapsack, and walked quietly and unhurriedly into the darkened bedroom. A light bloomed by the bedside as Mary's fumbling fingers found the elusive switch.

"Raine? Raine?" Mary's iteration of her name held elements of beginning panic.

"I'm here, Mary," came Raine's swiftly soothing reassurance. "I was reading in the living room."

"I . . . I thought you'd left!"

"I won't leave until you're able to cope on your own, Mary," Raine promised her firmly.

"Truly?"

"Truly."

Mary sank back against her pillows in relief and tears began to well in her eyes and slide down her cheeks. Raine acted promptly to distract her from a threatened emotional storm which could help neither Mary nor her situation.

"I don't know about you, but I'm ravenous, Mary," she said briskly. "How about our putting room service on its toes and have them send up some food worthy of our discerning taste buds? This hotel's restaurant is famous for its fresh seafood and I can always eat my weight in crab." She smiled encouragingly and Mary responded with a tremulous effort of her own that grew stronger and more natural as Raine's own smile widened approvingly.

They made their selections and while they were waiting for room service, Raine helped Mary to dress in a comfortable lounging robe, brush and arrange her disordered hair, and generally repair the ravages of the taxing events of the day.

Over the excellent dinner they talked—Raine, distractingly, about some of her experiences in the beautiful and the barren corners of the world she had explored. She had seen the sun rise over the deserts and set into the oceans, had smelled the sulfurous fumes of the breath of a volcano and the delicate scent of a dew-misted posy of flowers picked for her by a shy young shepherd in a mountain valley. Only when she had determined that Mary had eaten and relaxed sufficiently did she allow the conversation to veer into subjects directly bearing on Mary's concerns.

"Tell me about your family, Mary. Have you children?" It was the first personal question Raine had asked and Mary recognized it as a delicate permission to discuss the subject uppermost on her mind.

"I have a son," she responded immediately. "My husband is dead, but we were divorced long before he died." The hardening of her padded jawline was a subtle indication that it had not been an amicable divorce.

"Is your son married?" Raine probed lightly. The right kind of wife would be a great help in a situation like this.

"No." There was a wealth of bitterness and guilt in that quiet negative. "Between us, I think Tony and I destroyed Nick's taste for marriage. He has 'friends,' not a wife, and though I suppose Nick cares for me because I'm his mother, his opinion of women is not noticeably favorable. Nick is a prototype for the original uncommitted male. Women come and go in his life. None last, none matter. He was a loving, affectionate child, but he's become a hard, cynical man. Of course the people he associates with would make a saint cynical," Mary stated wryly. "Among his various enterprises is a resort hotel on the Nevada side of Lake Tahoe. It's his main base of operations and he and I have permanent suites in the hotel. I live there practically year round, except for short trips to follow the sun when the winter cold gets to be too much for my old bones. I usually take a cruise through the Panama Canal to the Caribbean to bake the chill out of my marrow at least once in deep winter."

While Mary reminisced silently about previous cruises, Raine's thoughts were running on far different lines. Her previous experiences while traveling the world had taught her to think several steps ahead and to examine carefully all possible consequences of any proposed course of action.

Her immediate reaction to Mary's summation of her son's character was dismay and distaste. Raine had been raised, and loved, in a tradition of faithful men, whose steadfast devotion was matched in full measure by an equal devotion from their chosen women. Her instinctive response to the promiscuous, predatory male was contemptuous, often explicitly so when persistently importuned by uninvited advances. Raine had traveled alone for five years. She had become expert in repelling unwanted attentions.

Although Mary hadn't yet broached the subject, Raine knew that soon she would ask Raine to come to her home, to stay with her for a while. Raine had developed an inner serenity and strength that Mary could draw on to help her through the coming days. Whether Raine accepted the invitation would depend on several factors, one of which could be settled immediately.

"Mary, does Nick have a current 'friend'?" she asked hopefully. If his attention were already firmly fixed, she would have one less problem to cope with. Raine wasn't at all vain, but she was a realist. She was passably attractive, an understatement many men would have disputed, and men of Nick's general type usually saw a new woman as a challenge. She had no desire to upset Mary by having to obviously repel advances from her son.

"Oh, yes, Nick has a current mistress." Mary abruptly dispensed with her previous euphemism. "Her name is Selene Eason and she's as cold and icy a beauty as the moon she named herself for. She sings in the lounge at the hotel and her stage name is just as false as her platinum hair. She'd like to become Mrs. Nicholas Anthony Hunter, but all she'll ever be is a short-talent cabaret singer!" Mary's dismissive words clearly indicated what she thought of Selene's aspirations . . . all of them!

Raine didn't care what Selene Eason's chances were in the matrimonial or the entertainment stakes, just as long as she had enough talent to keep Nick Hunter occupied and off the prowl! She could have full rights to him with Raine's enthusiastic blessing, sight unseen.

"Raine?" Mary's hesitant pronunciation of her name recalled Raine's wandering attention. Mary's hands were twisting and clenching in her lap as she nerved herself to ask a further, greater, favor from the young woman who had done so much for her already.

"Yes, Mary?" Raine smiled encouragingly.

"You . . . you said you wouldn't leave me until I was able to cope on my own. Did you mean it? Will you come and stay a while? I . . . I need time to . . . to learn how to die." She burst into tears.

Raine swept around the table in a flash. She gently assisted the weeping woman over to the nearby couch and sat with her there, holding her with strong young arms until the racking sobs eased. When the silent comfort of human contact had soothed the unhappy woman, Raine spoke sincerely.

"I'll come with you to Tahoe, Mary. I'll come, but I won't help you to die. I'll help you to live."

Long after Mary had found brief oblivion in sleep, Raine sat alone in the shadow-filled living room of the hotel suite, staring down the corridors of memory. Would she truly have the stamina to go through with this? Could she become Mary's strength in the dark times, when the spirit falters and the fight is resigned? It would mean reopening the old scars of

26

five years ago, scars which had closed, but which were still exquisitely painful to direct probing.

For five years Raine had fashioned an existence without Johnny and it had been, in many ways, a fulfilling life. Now, if she were to give of her best in answer to Mary's appeal, she must be prepared to endure the resurgent echoes of the old searing agony. She had promised to help Mary learn to live. Had she the courage to withstand the pressures of present grief and past sorrows? Dare she try?

But in the end, there was no choice. She had given her word and it was not in her to walk away from *un cri de coeur.*

The next morning as they lingered at breakfast, Raine asked, "Does your son know why you came to San Francisco, Mary?"

"No, he doesn't," Mary admitted. "He thinks I came to do some shopping and to see some plays. I've been seeing a specialist in Reno and he sent me to Stanford for the tests. Nick doesn't know anything about it."

"You'll have to tell him. He has the right to know." Raine stated the obvious.

"I know," Mary admitted. "He's my son. He has the right to know, but . . . but not yet, Raine. I don't want him to know yet."

Raine made an instinctive motion of disagreement. The situation was distressing enough without the addition of some foolish intrigue. Nick Hunter, whatever his moral maturity, was nonetheless an adult male and his mother was a dying woman. It was madness to try to shield him from the realities of life!

"It's not for his sake, Raine." Mary had deciphered Raine's expression easily. "Please try to understand. It's for my sake. I . . . I feel that I must first come to terms with what's happening to me before I can bear to have anyone else know, especially Nick. I haven't been a very good mother to him, I'm afraid. I've failed him badly in so many ways, but I want, for his sake and my own, to die well. What was the saying? 'Nothing in his life became him like the leaving it.' I can bear it if *you* see me cry and curse at fate, but I don't want Nick to know until I'm sure I won't go all to pieces. I haven't any gift left to give him except that of meeting death with dignity."

It was an appeal with no recourse. Raine could only acquiesce, but she did so with the mental proviso that once she had met Nick Hunter, she would make her own decision about when and how much he should be told. She wasn't going to be bound by a blind promise if breaking it would help Mary Hunter. Nick Hunter's sensibilities weren't her concern!

Mary evidently took her silence for consent, if not total agreement, and went on to discuss the travel arrangements. "I usually fly into Reno and Nick sends a car for me or comes himself if he's free. Why don't you check to be sure that there's space on today's flight, although it shouldn't be a problem since there are usually plenty of seats. If, by some chance, the flight's full, we can always stay over another day." She hesitated momentarily and went on with a slightly embarrassed air. "I'll be responsible for all of your travel and other expenses, Raine,

28

and of course you'll be my guest at the resort. There are guest rooms and suites in the family wing."

Raine looked at Mary blankly for a moment and then a husky chuckle of pure amusement gurgled in her throat. She looked down at her clean but well-worn jeans and her grin was tinged with rueful good humor. "That's very sweet of you, Mary, and I do suppose that I might easily be taken for an impecunious ragamuffin, but I assure you that I'm not down to my last penny. I've just traveled up from Mexico on a tramp freighter and before that I stayed at a small village in the Baja for a month and a half. Believe me, jeans were both practical and comfortable at that time. I sent my other clothes home when I decided to stay in Mexico for a while because I travel light whenever I can. I'll do some shopping when I get to Tahoe. As for the other, well thank you for the offer and the thought behind it, but I pay my own way. I always have. I'm coming to Tahoe as your friend, nothing more."

Raine's smile was so sweet and her voice so gentle that there was no offense in the refusal. Mary accepted the gentle rejection easily, laughing, in her turn, as she remembered. "Of course, I keep forgetting. I've seen the price stickers on your works, when they're available, in the galleries. I just can't seem to accept that you're *Talbot.*"

"I'm not Talbot, Mary," Raine reminded her. "I'm Raine Fisher, your friend. Talbot is a name in a gallery, on a canvas, or a sketch, not a real person at all. Only Raine Fisher comes to Tahoe with you."

Raine's meaning was clear. Only Raine Fisher, a young woman she had met by chance, would accom-

29

pany Mary Hunter. Talbot would remain locked away with the treasures concealed in the portfolio that was Raine's constant companion.

"I suppose that I can't tell Nick how you saved my life either." Mary accepted Raine's decision with a touch of mischief.

"Good lord, no!" Raine objected vigorously. "Must we explain anything at all for the time being? Won't he just accept me as your guest? A friend you met in San Francisco and impulsively asked to visit you? I don't think anything else is his business."

"Well, we can try it." Mary grimaced with ill-concealed doubt. "But Nick thinks most things *are* his business. He's a very forceful man, Raine, and very much in command of his surroundings."

And he's not the trusting sort . . . Raine mentally tallied another trait, adding it to her growing mosaic of the unknown Nick's character, most of it based on his mother's unconscious revelations and her own previous experience with men of his ilk. She normally went out of her way to avoid prejudgment, but this time it seemed that she'd be hard put to look at Nick Hunter with anything but jaundiced eyes.

To be blunt, her position was going to be equivocal. Mary didn't want her son to know the truth about her medical condition. Raine was adamant about refusing to use the name and persona of Talbot to lend herself an air of respectability, and Nick Hunter sounded like the type of man to put the worst possible construction on her motives for accompanying his mother to Tahoe.

Well, it couldn't be helped, and Raine frankly

couldn't have cared less what an unknown man, one she was already predisposed to dislike, thought about her, as long as it didn't adversely affect his mother's well being.

CHAPTER II

With the easy expertise of a seasoned traveler, Raine smoothed their departure from the hotel and obtained transportation to the airport. Her commanding eye contact with a lounging skycap relieved them of the burden of Mary's suitcases, both of which were checked through because they were too large to fit beneath the plane's seats. Raine's knapsack was slung casually over her shoulders as carry-on luggage, being of a size to slide easily beneath the seat in front of her. Her portfolio would repose in the overhead . . . it was never far from her hand at any time. The major canvases had gone home by other means, but the preliminary sketches and color notes for projected paintings were irreplaceable. There were also several series of pen and ink drawings which would make Ray Denton, the gallery owner who acted as her agent, rub his hands with glee.

Raine declined the honor of the window seat, having already seen too many miles pass beneath her while flying, to be intrigued by the view between San Francisco and Reno. The short flight precluded meal service, but Raine and Mary munched contentedly on hickory-smoked and salted almonds and sipped ginger ale. The man in the aisle seat rapidly downed two Bloody Marys with the practiced aplomb of a seasoned drinker and initiated a conversation with the ease of a practiced flirt. Raine rebuffed his overtures deftly but politely since he didn't persist or make a nuisance of himself.

After they had deplaned at Reno, Raine lagged behind while she hoisted the knapsack into place and eased the straps across her shoulders to balance the load comfortably. Mary had walked several steps ahead while Raine was occupied with this somewhat awkward operation, thus giving Raine an unimpeded view of the reunion between mother and son.

Hunter by name, hunter by nature. If she had been asked to describe him with one word, Raine would have chosen *dangerous.* There was very little to mark him, physically, as Mary Hunter's son. She was softly, self-indulgently plump; he was disciplined and tautly lean. Where some men might have been characterized as broadswords, clubbing and crushing opposition, and others as rapiers, dispatching with graceful, flexible finesse, Nick Hunter was a sabre, deadly in the thrust and parry.

There would be other men physically taller and broader of shoulder than he, but few could match him in a competition he chose to enter, if he judged that the prize was worth his interest. He was a survivor, a cynic, and never a saint. He took what he wanted, but he paid for it, and the first price he had paid had been the loss of all innocence and illusions. He was probably only five or six years older than Raine herself, but more than years separated them.

Raine wondered if Hunter was an anglicized ver-

34

sion of an American Indian name, because a coppery tone underlay the tanned skin that was stretched tautly over the high cheekbones and hawklike nose, and there was a raven-black sheen to the straight thick hair that lapped over his ears and conformed to the back of his neck. His eyes were dark beneath the shelf of his brows, so dark a brown that they were nearly black. His mouth smiled at his mother, but when the smile faded, his lips rested in a straight, almost cruel, line of control.

The brief formality of greeting was over and he placed his hand beneath Mary's elbow to escort her to the baggage claim area. Raine, still the detatched observer, waited calmly for Mary to inform him of the addition of an unexpected (and unwelcome?) third to their party. His unguarded first reaction to her inclusion would be illuminating and, to a large measure, would probably set the whole tone of their future relationship . . . stormy or smoothly neutral.

Raine had no desire to provoke a reaction more positive than that of cooperative neutrality from Mary's son. Her perceptive artist's eye had made its own evaluation of his character, totally independent of any preconceptions she might have already formulated based on Mary's previous revelations concerning her son's character. In Nick Hunter's face Raine saw strength, arrogance, and cynical detatchment. What softer emotions he might once have experienced had long since been locked away behind an impregnable barrier and she hadn't the slightest desire to search for a key to fit its lock. She would do what she could for Mary and then she would move on, back into the mainstream of her life, without a backward glance toward Nick Hunter.

"Just a moment, Nick, dear." Mary resisted the gentle compulsion of Nick's guiding hand. "I've brought a friend with me. The green suite is available, isn't it?"

He immediately halted and scanned the area behind them, searching for his mother's traveling companion. His eyes passed over Raine, widening slightly in an automatic masculine appreciation of her face and attractively curved figure, but dismissing her attire with a contemptuous flick of his dark eyes.

Perhaps it was the fact that there was no one else near their small group—the other passengers had long since streamed past, intent on their own pressing concerns—or perhaps it was the mockingly amused expression that Raine had not attempted to conceal, but his gaze returned to her with an almost audible snap.

Mary innocently confirmed his suspicions. She held out a beckoning hand to Raine, drawing her forward to present her to a grim-faced Nick. "Nick, dear, I'd like you to meet a *very* dear friend, Raine Fisher," and artlessly made bad worse by adding, "Raine must have the best we have to offer, Nick."

Raine was torn between a desire to groan and one to laugh harder than she ever had before in her life. There was, however, no sign of laughter on Nick Hunter's face.

He swept an insultingly comprehensive glance up and down from her head to her toes, and acknowledged formally, "Miss Fisher." There was no welcoming warmth in the clipped syllables.

Raine matched his glance and his tone and responded, "*Mrs.* Fisher, Mr. Hunter."

His glance at her ringless left hand was expressive, but his coldly polite "*Mrs.* Fisher" accepted the correction.

Raine had removed the wedding rings from her finger and Johnny's after his death and they now reposed in a small chamois bag in her jewelry case that was stored at her parents' home. She had needed no visible reminders symbolic of their marriage . . . it had its own reality in her mind. She owed no explanation to Nick Hunter.

"I'm afraid that the green suite isn't available," Nick informed his mother. His voice was absolutely without inflection.

So, no cooperation, no neutrality, Raine thought scornfully. Evidently, to Nick Hunter, clothes made the woman. He had dismissed her jeans and shirt, and the woman who wore them, with an instantaneous evaluation. Raine firmly suppressed a lamentable urge to laugh in his face. She really didn't give a tinker's damn what he thought of her. The long years of independence and travel plus a clear-sighted recognition of the worth of her talent had made Raine reliant on no one's good opinion save her own. She would have lived to please Johnny. Now she lived to please herself. Nick Hunter's approval or disapproval meant nothing to her and unless he upset his mother, he could be as censorious as he pleased, to her face or behind her back!

"Why isn't the green suite available, Nick?" Mary

queried sharply. She hadn't missed Nick's silent reaction to Raine.

"Because it's already occupied," he explained blandly. "I thought Selene might be more comfortable in a suite since her contract with the lounge has been extended and she was feeling rather cramped in the staff quarters."

And presumably it was one of the perks of the "job" to be moved into more luxurious quarters if the owner decided to extend the length of her singing engagement? Or more convenient? From what Mary had said, the green suite was situated close to or within the family section of the hotel. Selene Eason had evidently made a success of *all* aspects of her career, Raine concluded with concealed relief. Nick Hunter would be otherwise occupied.

"But I want Raine to be near me," Mary objected. "There aren't any other unoccupied suites on our floor and I don't want her put into just a single room."

Mary was becoming agitated and Raine felt it was time for her to take a hand in the proceedings. "Mary." She spoke with quiet authority, and the older woman looked to her immediately for guidance. "A single room will be fine. I'll be very comfortable." Her tone conveyed both gentle reassurance and inflexible command. Mary subsided obediently. If Raine didn't care to make an issue of the size of her accommodations, Mary wouldn't press the subject.

Raine switched her attention back to a speculative Nick Hunter, who hadn't missed a word of the exchange between his mother and this unknown woman. He was scowling. He hadn't liked Mary's abrupt capitulation to Raine's dictum. It was totally out of character. Mary was fond of having her own way and opposition had always made her obstinate, not amenable.

"I'm sure that there's a single room not too far from your mother's suite, Mr. Hunter?" Only the very faintest of inflections transformed it into a question, rather than an order.

"I'm sure we can find a suitable accommodation for you, Mrs. Fisher," Nick agreed noncommittally.

"I'm sure you can," Raine murmured, and dropped her gaze to hide her dancing eyes. A refurbished broom closet, no doubt! Well, it wouldn't have a mud floor, which was all her previous abode had boasted.

They were the last passengers from their flight to claim their baggage. Nick spotted his mother's two suitcases immediately and, waving away a porter, hefted them himself. With a cool politeness he asked Raine, "Which are yours?"

"I have it," she responded briefly, gesturing at the knapsack that now rode easily on her back and the portfolio tucked carefully beneath her arm.

"You travel light." It wasn't a compliment.

"Sometimes." Raine wouldn't be drawn.

They headed south from the city on the broad divided highway, U.S. 395, but soon angled southwesterly onto the narrower state highway, climbing up into the cooler tree-clad heights in a remarkably short time.

Raine, comfortably ensconced on the back seat, enjoyed her first ground-level view of the deep jewel which was Lake Tahoe. It was lovely, and Raine could easily understand its appeal for so many people, in all seasons. It possessed a scenic allure which, ironically, threatened the life of the lake itself from ecological damage caused by the population explosion around its environs. People came, they saw, they wanted to stay, and too many of them had!

The hotel was no surprise to Raine. It was luxurious, expensive, and obviously efficiently managed. It lacked a soul. People would come to gamble, and in the winter season, to gambol on the slopes, and, afterward, to risk more than a broken bone in the après ski. She could not live for long in such a place without feeling stifled. She decided that she might almost prefer the discomfort and privation of a mud hut to the impersonality of a lushly carpeted, sterile chamber, no matter how elegantly appointed.

Nick must have sensed something of her opinion, but had misinterpreted the reasons behind her stiff appraisal of her surroundings. When they paused before the door of Mary's suite he said smoothly, "I'll show Mrs. Fisher to her room, Mary. She can join you after she's unpacked and has had a chance to freshen up."

"That's fine, Nick, dear," Mary agreed. It was time for her medication and she wanted to stretch out on her bed and wait for it to take effect. Raine would understand.

Raine did. Mary needed privacy. Nick Hunter thought he needed privacy too, because he wouldn't want an audience, especially one which contained his mother, while he tried to interrogate and intimidate his mother's "guest." Raine was prepared to grant both of their wishes.

"I'll see you later, Mary." Raine smiled at her reassuringly. Mary disappeared after a brief farewell and grateful smile. The bellhop followed her into the suite, a suitcase in each hand.

Nick led the way to a door some distance down the corridor from Mary's suite. Raine trailed him obediently, a docile two paces behind. Her downcast eyes concealed her expression from Nick. The next few minutes should be interesting, Raine thought.

He opened the door with a master key and stood back to allow her to enter first, as befitted a proper host. Raine preceded him and walked into the nearly dark room. With the precision of a night-seeing cat she advanced farther into the room, guided by the small amount of light that filtered through the double thickness of the curtains and the artificial light from the outer corridor. Even that doubtful source of illumination was extinguished when he closed the door behind them with a definitive click.

Raine swiveled to face him, her face absolutely still, schooled to betray neither apprehension nor surprise at his unorthodox behavior. Harsh light from an overhead fixture flooded the room when he flicked a switch located by the door leading to the hall, and revealed them, as though spotlighted on a stage set, ready to play their parts and speak their lines with conviction and passion.

Raine glanced calmly around, slipped the knapsack from her shoulders, and tossed it onto the queen-size bed that dominated the spacious room. She carefully placed her portfolio atop the mirrored dresser and faced Nick again, slipping her thumbs into the front belt loops of her jeans while she waited for him to speak.

If he admired her unflustered poise it didn't show on his hard face as he lounged back against the closed door. His arms were crossed over his chest, but there was nothing casual about the obsidian glitter of his dark eyes.

Stare for stare she matched him, the blue depth of her eyes against the inquisition of his silent appraisal as it battered, prodded, and probed, searching for her slightest weakness. She watched him with an artist's detachment which armed her against what might have been an otherwise unnerving assault.

Abruptly he abandoned the silent visual confrontation for another tactic. "Where did you meet my mother?" he rapped out. "How long have you known her?"

If he had hoped to disconcert her with rapid-fire interrogation, he was due for another disappointment. "I met her in San Francisco," Raine replied with perfect composure. "Yesterday."

With an effort she suppressed the slightest of betraying grins. Really . . . he was almost amusingly predictable. A long-buried sense of mischief struggled briefly to the surface, and tantalizing possibilities flitted through her mind. If it weren't for the tragic circumstances, she would have enjoyed tying Mr. Nick Hunter into one king-size Gordian knot. But for Mary's sake she couldn't.

He waited for her to add some embellishment to her brief answers, but Raine was not to be caught in such a trap. Any information he managed to extract from her would be pared bone-thin, with no additional flesh to make a meal of speculation. Raine was well practiced in the art of protecting her privacy, and it had become second nature to parry questions automatically.

"You've only known my mother a day and yet she's invited you to visit her for a stay of unspecified duration?" His deep voice was filled with deliberately insulting disbelief and suspicion.

"Yes." The attempt at insult couldn't touch her. After all, he spoke the simple truth. She *had* met Mary just over twenty-four hours ago.

Her monosyllabic answer seemed to enrage him. With a rippling thrust of his shoulders he abandoned the lounging pose he had assumed against the door and, with three long strides, he moved to confront her, glaring down into her widening eyes. Her first assessment of him had been accurate. He was dangerous.

"What do you hope to gain, Mrs. Fisher? Are you looking for a soft berth and a free ride?" he growled, dark menace threading each word.

She tilted her head back so that she could meet his eyes fairly and diced with danger one more time, daring to answer his questions with just one, unadorned word.

"No."

His hard hands clamped down suddenly on her shoulders. A fraction more pressure would be bruising, so she didn't struggle against his strength. She wouldn't fight him on a physical level.

"I don't believe you, Mrs. Fisher," he spat out through clenched teeth. "I saw the way you looked

43

around the hotel and I think you've a fancy to enjoy the luxurious life for a while, courtesy of my mother. You're obviously not accustomed to these surroundings, nor prepared for them." His eyes flicked over her clothes again, emphasizing his meaning. "I think that tomorrow you'd better tell my mother that you've changed your mind and have decided to travel on to your original destination. I'll even drive you to the nearest bus station and buy your ticket." The rail was ready, all that was lacking was the tar and feathers.

"Take your hands off my shoulders, Mr. Hunter," Raine said icily. She was not amused any longer and between one heartbeat and the next an amazing metamorphosis occurred. Subtly, in a way he could not have described, Raine's demeanor changed dramatically, and Nick's hands involuntarily lifted from her shoulders and fell to his sides. A hard flush ran beneath his skin in response to the freezing contempt that showed so plainly in her eyes. He didn't know it, but he was now face-to-face with *Talbot*, and an angry Talbot, an arrogant Talbot, at that!

" 'I'll be judge, I'll be jury,' said cunning old Fury, 'I'll try the whole cause, and condemn you to death.' Is that it, Mr. Hunter? I'm judged unsuitable to associate with your mother. I'm to be bought off with a bus ticket." She drew in a deep breath. "Who made *you* God, Nicholas Hunter, that you presume to condemn me on the strength of a few hours' acquaintance? Who I am, where I come from and where I'll go when I leave here, all are none of your business! Your mother is a grown woman and fully capable of choosing her own friends and companions. Because

I care about her I will say this much to you. No harm will come to your mother through me. You have my word." She pinned him with a glare, spacing her next words. "Now have my warning. Do not meddle further or seek to make trouble between your mother and me or you will regret it for the rest of your life." She held up an admonitory hand. "No, I'm your mother's guest, but I'm not *yours.* When the time comes for me to leave this place, you may be assured that my bill will be paid in full. That being the case, I expect to enjoy the courtesy due any paying guest, which is the privacy of the room I'm paying for." She walked over to the door, opened it, and pronounced harshly, "Get out!"

He left. She slammed the door behind him. Then she threw herself down on the bed and shook from sheer outrage and temper. No one, no one had ever spoken to her in such a way! He had literally tried to run her out of town. Damn his arrogance and his holier-than-thou attitude!

When the worst effects of the temper fit had passed, Raine reached for the bedside phone and contacted housekeeping. She requested that an ironing board and an iron be sent to her room as soon as possible.

She hadn't been this angry, in a personal sense, in years. During her travels she had often been moved to anger and to tears because of the things she had seen, but it had had nothing to do with her most deeply guarded emotions, emotions she had kept locked away since Johnny's death. She had sometimes been in danger of her life, had been afraid, cold, lonely. She had laughed as well, had been touched by

45

kindness and beauty, but there had always been a layer of feeling that nothing could reach, an innermost citadel that had been sealed away when Johnny had left this world. She hadn't even consciously been aware of its existence, so deeply buried had that knot of feelings lain, but now, with that scalding rush of anger, she knew that Nick Hunter had crashed through an indefinable barrier, making her feel unexpectedly and uncomfortably vulnerable. She didn't like the sensation.

She began to unpack a miscellany of things from her knapsack and, had there been a witness to the growing pile of clothes, shoes, and other objects, all of which came forth from seemingly bottomless depths, he might well have rubbed his eyes in disbelief. How she could have gotten so much into so little space was destined to remain a trade secret.

By the time she had managed to transfer most of her clothes into the drawers and to otherwise arrange the rest of her possessions, a tap on the door announced the arrival of the items she had requested. She tipped the messenger with a bill and a smile. He went away happy.

Raine set up the ironing board, plugged in the iron after shaking it to ascertain that some thoughtful person had already filled it with water, and set the temperature on "cotton." While it was heating, she walked over to the bed and shook open a bundle of fabric that had been rolled into a tight cylinder. It was a dress.

Tomorrow she would shop to augment her wardrobe, but tonight she would need a dress. They'd be dining in the hotel's main restaurant—Mary had described it during the flight—and jeans were definitely not *de rigueur* in such surroundings. The dress she was holding would be suitable . . . and more.

The fabric was coarse Mexican cotton, dyed a slate blue, but the design and the intricate hand embroidery made it a work of art. Raine had designed and commissioned it and several other items during her stay in Mexico and a couturier would have sold his soul to have been able to put his name on any or all of them.

The lines of the dress were simple—the low, square-necked bodice was banded beneath the bosom with a broad repeat of the embroidered motif that edged the neckline, sleeve hem, and hemline. The décolletage was designed to expose a smoothly tanned expanse of throat, shoulder, and rising swell of breast, provocative packaging that promised much but revealed only tantalizing hints. The sleeves were elbow length and flared. The long skirt fell in a graceful flow to the floor, having been attached with soft gathers beneath the high, tight bodice, except for a straight-hanging, flat panel directly in front. It was about seven inches wide beneath the breasts but gradually widened until it was almost eighteen inches across at the hem. On this panel had been embroidered an enlarged and simplified version of the detailed pattern that edged the hems.

While she carefully ironed the dress Raine muttered, "*Now* judge a person by the clothes she wears, Nick Hunter."

Raine and Mary had a late lunch in Mary's suite.

When they were nearly finished, Mary asked bluntly, "What's your impression of Nick?"

"I find him physically impressive," Raine admitted. "He's all you said he was, forceful, dynamic and . . ." she grinned ". . . cynical."

Mary winced. "You've already had a run-in with him."

"Yes, but don't worry," Raine reassured her lightly. "The honors were even. Neither of us inflicted a fatal wound."

Mary didn't smile. Her mouth had a disconsolate droop and her eyes were wistful. "I—I had hoped that, in spite of everything, you'd like him. You don't like him, do you, Raine?"

Raine had long since decided that there must be only truth between them if she were to be able to help Mary. It was not the time for polite fictions of any sort. Mary must come to accept life as it was, not as she hoped it might be. "No," Raine said gently, "I don't like him particularly. But, Mary, it isn't necessary that I like him. I am your friend. All that is necessary between Nick and me is that we maintain a civil relationship. It would be easier if we told him why I have come to stay with you for a while, but I can contrive until you decide that the time is right to tell him."

"But, Raine, I wanted you to like him," Mary wailed softly. "You'd be so right for him . . ." She clapped a horrified hand across her mouth to block further indiscreet revelations.

Raine stared at the woman across the table with appalled comprehension. "My God, Mary! You haven't been *matchmaking!*"

Mary's blush was confirmation enough for Raine. Raine didn't know whether to laugh or to cry.

She did neither. She tried to explain the impossibility of such a notion as tactfully as possible. "Mary, you must understand. I had a husband whom I loved very much. When he died, my world splintered into a million pieces and it has taken me a long, long time to rebuild it in some acceptable form. I—I have gotten used to being a rover, to traveling the world, painting and recording new places and people. My family ties pull me home now and again, but I have shaped my life along other lines from those it would have taken had Johnny and I had more time, had we had a normal span. I can't bring back the past and so I live in the present. I had a husband. Now I have a career." It was as gentle a rejection as she could devise.

"And Nick is not like your Johnny," Mary said softly.

"No, Nick is not like my Johnny." Raine's voice held an aching softness whenever she spoke Johnny's name. She would never speak another man's name with just that same tender inflection.

"Nick needs you, Raine." Mary was stubbornly determined. Now that her schemes were exposed and her machinations laid bare, there could be no further harm in explaining her reasoning.

"I did Nick a great wrong once. I told you that Tony and I were divorced long before he died. What I didn't tell you, although you might have inferred it, was that our marriage was a hell on earth. I loved Tony when I married him, or perhaps it might be more accurate to say that I desired him, only we

49

didn't admit to it so blatantly in those days. Anyway, we got married. We had to. Nick was on the way. Our parents, his and mine, forced Tony to marry me. He resented it and he punished me for it every day of our marriage. I was jealous and possessive and so his punishment took the form of other women. A legion of other women."

Mary's face twisted with old pain. Raine stretched out a comforting hand across the table that Mary grasped gratefully, squeezed, and released before she continued with her narrative.

"I kept it from Nick. He knew that we didn't have a happy marriage, Tony and I. You can't hide those things from a child. But he didn't know why. Tony finally killed my love—my desire, if you will—with his constant infidelities, and at last I turned to another man for a little tenderness, and, perhaps, to hit back at Tony as well."

She sighed and pressed her temples as though they ached. In an infinitely weary voice she continued. "That affair was disastrous, and the person it hurt most was Nick. He was ten. He walked in on Jack and me in bed together one afternoon. He had gotten sick at school and came home early. I'll never forget his face." She buried her head in her shaking hands. Raine sat in silent sympathy. There was nothing she could say.

Finally Mary was able to continue. "Soon afterward Tony and I were divorced. Not because of Jack —Tony wouldn't have cared if I had slept with a hundred men—but because I realized that we were destroying Nick. Nick asked to live with Tony. Tony refused. He didn't want the responsibility of a child.

I tried to make Nick understand that it wasn't that his father didn't *love* him, but . . ." She raised her hands in a helpless gesture and let them fall limply back to her lap. "How can you explain something like that to a child? And make him *believe* that it isn't his fault?"

Again there was no answer Raine could make.

"Nick stayed with me—there was nowhere else for him to go—and I tried to erase some of the damage, but he wouldn't let me close to him. I don't think he's ever trusted another woman from that day. As soon as he was old enough, he moved into his own apartment. When Tony died, he left everything to Nick, but I don't think Nick has ever touched a penny of it. By then he was making his own way, you see. He needed nothing from either of us." Mary looked at Raine with a mutely agonized plea for understanding.

"Nick is a man now, Mary. Have you ever tried to talk to him about your marriage? Children see in black and white. A man can see the shades of gray. A marriage is neither built nor destroyed by one person alone and perhaps you can help him to understand that now," Raine suggested.

Inwardly she was appalled. This was a complication she could never, in her worst nightmares, have foreseen. Mary had wanted to expiate her sins, real and imagined, and evidently had envisioned handing Raine to Nick as some sort of panacea, a cure-all for his disinclination to make a commitment to one and only one woman. If Mary persisted with this deluded notion, it would make Raine's sojourn at the hotel intolerable and impossible. She would not be thrown at a man she could neither respect nor like!

"I haven't tried to talk to Nick about his father and me since Tony died. I tried then, but Nick wouldn't hear of it. He'd said, 'Let the dead rest!' and I haven't had the courage to raise the subject since. When he bought controlling interest in the hotel, he offered me a suite. It was the first major overture he'd made toward me and I didn't want to do anything that would send him back into that hard, defensive shell he's cultivated over the years. I sold my condominium, invested the proceeds, and moved in. I've never regretted it, but, oh, Raine, I regret so many other things . . ." She burst into wracking sobs.

Raine began murmuring soothing phrases designed to calm the distraught woman and mentally cursed Nick Hunter. Perhaps he had been more sinned against than sinning when he was a child, but he was older, if not wiser, now. It was becoming uncomfortably clear that the relationship between mother and son was going to be one of the hardest factors to deal with and Raine had a horrible premonition that she was going to be the one who would have to at least start the reconciliation process.

When Mary's emotional tempest had abated, Raine reapproached the subject cautiously, attempting to defuse the emotional powder keg with dampening humor. "Mary, dear, you must realize that I can't be prescribed for Nick like some miracle drug, and I'm sure your son would consider me much too bitter a pill to swallow." She essayed a small grin and was relieved when Mary rolled her eyes heavenward and grimaced at the dreadful pun.

"I know, Raine," Mary admitted ruefully. "I should know by now that you can't command love. It's just . . . you're a woman who has known deep commitment. The women Nick associates with are committed only to themselves. I want something better than that for my son."

"But, Mary, you don't really know me as a person," Raine pointed out.

"I know the important things," Mary said stubbornly. "You're compassionate and kind. You have a sense of involvement with life. You're capable of great depths of feeling and if a man were lucky enough to have your love, no matter what life did to him, he'd still come up a winner. I wanted that for Nick, Raine."

Raine's face had grown progressively redder with each word and by the time Mary had finished, she was fiery with embarrassment. Here was plain speaking with a vengeance!

This time it was Mary who eased the situation, but there was no humor, only resigned acceptance in her voice when she continued. "I didn't mean to embarrass you, Raine, but I felt that I had to say what I think. I haven't time for polite evasions anymore. I can see, too, that I'm not being fair to you. I'm already asking for so much from you and I do realize that my situation is going to reopen a lot of old wounds. If I were a stronger woman, I'd send you on to your family, but I'm not able to do that yet. I must lean on your strength for a time, but already I can feel myself making adjustments that I would have thought beyond me mere days ago, before I met you. You've helped me so much already. . . . Well, what

I'm trying to say in such a floundering manner is that I know that you can't be expected to be the salvation of the whole Hunter family, such as it is. I won't throw you at Nick or vice versa. You have my word on it." Her eyes twinkled briefly. "But you will allow me my very private daydreams, won't you?"

"As long as they remain *private*, Mary, dear," Raine agreed with a dry grin of relief. Secretly she wished that all of Mary's aspirations concerning a relationship between Raine and her son had remained private! It was bad enough that Nick Hunter thought she was out for what she could get from his mother. She couldn't bear even to think about what he would do or say if he ever acquired the notion that she was after *him!* As it was, had she had any inkling of what Mary had been hoping for, Raine would have been on the first plane east, moral obligation or no.

Back in her room, soaking luxuriously in a sinfully deep tub of hot water, Raine considered what Mary had said. It was true. She had known deep commitment. She would never, in any way, deny or denigrate what she and Johnny had shared. But if Mary Hunter only knew it—the very depth of her commitment to Johnny was the greatest impediment to the possibility that she would ever seek a commitment of such completeness again. She could not imagine being able to experience such unity of spirit with someone other than Johnny and, having once experienced it, was unable and unwilling to settle for less. She and Johnny had had a commonality of upbringing, ideals, and goals. She and Nick Hunter had nothing in common. In the past five years Raine had proved to herself that she could find fulfillment through her art and emotional sustenance through her family ties. It would content her. She was no threat to Nick Hunter's peace of mind (or lack of it)!

She finished her bath, smoothed body lotion over every inch of skin she could reach, front and back, and dusted herself in a white cloud of scented powder. Her honey-colored tan was completely uniform except for the minuscule area around her buttocks that had been covered by her *cache-sexe*. The stretches of beach near the village had been deserted and private. The village adults had had no time for swimming and the children could not venture as far afield as Raine could go.

With nothing but the addition of a small amount of moisturizing cream, Raine's complexion glowed with the golden blush of an apricot. The faintest application of mascara to darken the gilt tips of her eyelashes and a brush of gray-blue eye shadow dramatized the blue depths of her eyes. Her lips were naturally richly shaded and she had long ago ceased bothering with colored lipsticks or glosses, especially since she invariably ate the color away within minutes of its fresh application. Another woman would have looked colorless—Raine's unadorned mouth somehow achieved an innate sophistication that couldn't be counterfeited from a tube. Raine set her personal style, she didn't follow someone else's.

Her hair was disciplined into the severe elegance of a French twist, a style not "in" but, like a Chanel suit, possessed of a timeless, classical purity which, for the woman with the proper bone structure, lifted merely pretty into the rarified realm of beautiful ones.

After Raine had slipped into the Mexican dress she had planned to wear and uncurled from the contortions necessary to enable her to close the back zipper, she checked her appearance in the mirror of the dresser. It didn't allow her a full-length view, but even taken in sections, she was satisfied. A greater contrast to her casual, admittedly scruffy, jeans would be harder to find. An ever-so-slightly maliciously mischievous smile curled at the corners of her mouth. She was ready to go to dinner and Nick Hunter might find that a small side dish of crow was on the menu!

CHAPTER III

Raine knocked softly at the door of Mary's suite. A muffled sound, which Raine deciphered as "Come in," was the only answer she received. She twisted the doorknob and pushed the suite door ajar.

"Raine, is that you?" Mary's voice was lifted to carry through from the bedroom.

"Yes, it is, Mary," Raine called and, remembering her own recent efforts added, "do you need help with a zipper?"

"I did, but I've just managed to do it myself," Mary responded as she came through the door into the living room. She was concentrating on fastening a button at her wrist and didn't look up at Raine at first. When she did, her mouth dropped open in the classic mime of shock.

"My, my," she said reverently, when she had found her voice again. The impact of Raine's transmutation from ragamuffin into poised sophisticate was considerable. Mary had been, unlike her son, able to see past the surface of Raine's casual mode of dress, but her deeper insight had in no way prepared her for the Raine who stood before her now.

Raine wore no jewelry. She needed none. The sun-

and moon-streaked gold of her hair and the deep sapphire of her eyes were sufficient ornamentation. She was a lily that needed no gilding. Mary's mouth curved into a wickedly anticipatory smile. Beside Raine's dynamic simplicity the gaudy artificiality of Selene Eason would appear tawdry and ever so slightly trashy. Mary could hardly wait.

When Mary looked at Raine, she suddenly understood the full range of the French phrases *savoir faire,* meaning self-confidence, sophistication in its purest sense, and *savoir vivre,* embodying the shades of elegance, social grace, and good breeding. Raine was a natural aristocrat of blood and bone, unconsciously regal, and secure in the inner certainty of her own worth. There was no driving need within her to impress others with her own importance, but they would recognize it just the same. It was going to be a very interesting evening.

It was.

Their progress through the lobby left a trail of admiring masculine and envious feminine glances in their wake. Raine was serenely oblivious. Mary was highly diverted. And when they reached the restaurant, the reaction of their table companions was all, and more, than Mary could have desired.

Mary and Raine were ushered past the ordinary mortals waiting patiently for a table by the august personage of the maître d' himself, as was Mary's right. She was, after all, the mother of the hotel's owner. But it was Raine who was tenderly seated by that same impressive gentleman, leaving Mary to the ministrations of a lesser personage.

Mary couldn't have cared less. She was too intent on not missing the slightest flicker of expression on the faces of their table companions. Nick and Selene had been deep in conversation while Raine and Mary were being escorted in royal procession to the table, so the full impact of Raine's new appearance was in no way blunted by distance.

Nick couldn't believe it was the same woman. The contemptuous candor of her blue eyes assured him it was. Selene had had no prior encounter that would enable her to compare Raine's previous and present appearance, but this woman certainly didn't match Nick's insulting descriptives! Selene didn't like other women at the best of times. She was going to *hate* this one!

Raine was imperturbable. Nick Hunter had allowed himself nothing so gauche as a double take, but she could read every small, betraying muscle flicker. His stunned incredulity soothed every hackle her feminine *amour propre* had raised. Her revenge was more than adequate. She dismissed him from her mind for the moment and turned her attention to the other woman at the table. She recognized the type immediately.

Selene Eason was voluptuous, sultry, and her hair was skillfully silver, but nonetheless bleached. It also wouldn't do to turn one's back on her in a dark alley. Raine couldn't judge the extent of her talent, but she could make a fair guess as to her song style—she would make love to the microphone and thus, by inference, to every male member of the audience. Her silver lamé dress followed every curve faithfully, and fortunately she still had adequate muscle tone because she certainly wasn't wearing a bra beneath the dress. She had all the equipment necessary to keep Nick Hunter's attention. Raine smiled warmly at her. Selene couldn't know it, but Raine wished her nothing but the best of luck.

She got no smile (nor probably any good wishes either!) in return. Selene's brown eyes were hostilely assessing. Nick found his voice and made brief introductions.

"Selene, allow me to introduce my mother's friend, Raine Fisher. Mrs. Fisher, may I present Selene Eason. Selene is a friend of mine." The significance of the emphasis on the word *friend* each time was obvious, disparaging in the former, intimate in the latter. Selene preened and threw Nick an archly suggestive glance designed to underline the intimacy.

Raine tried out another smile. "I'm very pleased to meet you, Miss Eason. I'm looking forward to hearing you sing later this evening."

Selene wasn't pleased to meet Raine, but she answered civilly enough. "Thank you." A thought obviously occurred to her. "How did you know I'm a singer? Have you heard me sing somewhere else? Or did Nick tell you about me?" It was hard to tell which affirmative answer would have pleased her most.

"No, I haven't had the pleasure of hearing you before, I'm afraid," Raine admitted with just the proper tone of regret. "I've been out of the country for quite some time and have only recently returned to the States. And I've just met Mr. Hunter. He hasn't had time to do more than welcome me to the hospitality of his hotel." Raine's voice and demeanor were guilelessly innocent. "Mary—" she inclined her head toward the older woman "—told me about you."

"Oh?" There was a wealth of suspicion in that one word. Selene had a very accurate idea of Mary Hunter's opinion of her.

Raine's smile was reassuring. "Oh, yes. I'm so glad that you've settled in for an extended stay here at the hotel. I'm certain that I'll thoroughly enjoy your performances."

Mary proved herself a lady. Not a flicker of anything but courteous interest in the conversation crossed her face. She neither choked nor coughed into the glass of water she was sipping. Even if her hopes for Nick were not to be realized, she was still getting a tremendous amount of entertainment from Raine's masterly manipulation of the situation. Selene hadn't a clue!

Nick, however, was not so naive. He realized that he had just been handed over to his mistress on a tarnished silver platter. Raine had all but announced that Selene was welcome to sole possession of his person and his passion, that she, Raine, had no designs on him and even less interest in him as a man.

Raine realized that there were certain dangers inherent in the course she had chosen to pursue, but, after meeting Selene, she had decided that the probable gains would be worth the risks. She ran the minimal risk of intriguing Nick Hunter by her obvious disinclination to contend with Selene for his attentions, but his opinion of her was already so negative that she felt she could dismiss that possibility. Nick Hunter wanted a woman who would warm his bed

61

but not his heart. He wouldn't expend much effort in pursuit of an obviously unwilling woman. There were too many willing ones around!

That meant that they would have only the one major area of contention. Nick didn't trust her motives for befriending his mother. Well, that was fair enough. The circumstances were certainly suspicious and would remain so until Mary felt she could tell Nick what he must know. Until that time she could easily bear his mistrust, much of which was based on his initial impression of her as some sort of reincarnated hippie.

Selene's ability to sense a nuance was limited. Mary had been correct—Selene hadn't a clue that she had just been handed *carte blanche* with Nick as far as Raine was concerned. She had seen the way Nick had stared at this admittedly striking-looking woman, and the intensity with which he was *still* regarding her. She knew that Mary Hunter didn't like her and could be counted on to further the interests of anyone but Selene Eason where her son was concerned. While their menu selections were being recorded by the senior waiter, she laid out a campaign plan.

Raine was lifting a brimming glass of Weibel Green Hungarian to her lips when Selene's silkily insinuative voice said ruminatively, "*Mrs.* Fisher . . ." She arched a knowing eyebrow at a suddenly attentive Raine. "Will *Mr.* Fisher be joining you later?"

Mary stifled an appalled gasp. Raine's hand was steady as she lowered her glass to the table before answering. Her face was absolutely expressionless, but her eyes made Selene recoil involuntarily. "No." The flat negative forbade further probing.

Raine lifted the wineglass again, took a moderate sip, rolled it on her tongue, and observed conversationally, "I find that the quality of California table wines has steadily improved each time I return to the States, Mr. Hunter. In general I am of the opinion that the common California wines are superior to the *vin ordinaire* of almost any country and they match well against the premier wines as well." The only sign of her inner turmoil was the slightly pedantic phrasing of her sentences.

Nick ignored the proffered gambit of a noncontroversial discussion of wine. He chose instead to focus on another aspect of what she had said. "You sound as though you have done a considerable amount of traveling abroad."

"I have."

The arrival of the waiter bearing their first course interrupted what he was going to say next. The cream of asparagus soup was excellent. Nick looked as though he suspected that his had been made with grasshoppers. Selene kept him well occupied between sips, chattering about inconsequential subjects that nevertheless managed to exclude Mary and Raine. Raine enjoyed her soup and Mary enjoyed the by-play.

The service was excellent. As soon as they had finished one course, the plates were whisked away and others were presented with a flourish. The salad, freshly tossed at the table, their entrees, each different, each aromatically delicious, and, finally, the dessert cart, a cholesterol counter's nightmare, with enough whipped cream to keep every cow within a hundred miles laboring.

Raine feasted. There wasn't a tortilla or frijole in sight. She enjoyed Mexican food, and Italian pasta, and German cooking. In fact, she could eat almost any type of cuisine *con gusto,* but the menu at the small village had been somewhat limited, although nutritionally adequate. If she didn't see another bean or corn in any form, for some time, she wouldn't mind at all.

Selene declined coffee after Nick reminded her that she had to get ready for the show. She seemed particularly reluctant to leave Nick with Raine, in spite of the fact that Raine had endeavored, by all the subtle signs so well known and recognized by women, to assure the other woman that she was prepared to honor Selene's claim to him. Perhaps Selene might have been prepared to believe Raine, but she obviously didn't trust Nick. He spoke to Selene, but he watched Raine.

Nick rose courteously when Selene left the table, but he was oblivious to her hints that he escort her to her dressing room as was evidently his custom. Her slinky slither held more than a touch of frustrated irritation, but her dress was too tight and constricting to her stride to enable her to stalk off with the proper high dudgeon.

Nick didn't watch her go. He sank back into his seat, and Raine prepared herself for the resumption of his interrupted cross-examination. He got right down to it.

"I'm interested in hearing more about your travels, Raine." Raine's eyebrows quirked at the sudden intimacy of using her first name. The look she gave him was cool and direct, watchful but not intimidated.

"You don't mind if I call you Raine, do you?" Nick asked politely. "I can hardly continue to remain on such formal terms with a friend of my mother's."

Raine could tell that he expected nothing but polite acquiescence to his pro-forma request, and for a moment she imagined his expression should she insist on retaining the formality of her last name. It tempted her to refuse just to watch his face, but she sternly disciplined her errant impulses. It wasn't really worth the effort.

"Of course you may call me Raine." She gave gracious permission, but he could not help but realize that he had gained nothing. If he had thought to move inside of her defenses slightly, he had failed singularly.

"You will call me Nick?" he pressed, determined to force some response.

"If you wish." She gave him nothing, holding him easily at bay before her impassive indifference.

Neither had glanced at Mary during this exchange and she was content to maintain her low profile as observer. She wasn't sure just what Nick hoped to accomplish, but it was obvious to Mary that he was having heavy weather of it! She had been prepared to intervene on Raine's behalf if necessary, but it was now manifest that if anyone needed help, it was Nick, because he wasn't getting anywhere. She hadn't enjoyed herself so much in years. The more interest, from whatever motives, Nick showed in Raine, the happier Mary was.

Before Nick could consolidate whatever gain he might have made, Raine drew Mary smoothly into the conversation, sending her a mock-reproachful glance as she did so. She knew all too well what desires motivated Mary, but for the moment they could do no harm. Mary would need a distraction occasionally to lighten the burden she bore, a diversion to turn her thoughts away from her personal problems. If she wanted to nurture hopes about the possibility of a relationship between Nick and herself, Raine didn't really mind. Mary would soon realize the futility of her wishes and concentrate on a more attainable goal—a warmer relationship with her son.

With somewhat less than gentlemanly amiability Nick was forced to allow Raine to direct the channels of conversation into a discussion of the various summer activities available in the Reno-Tahoe area. She frustrated his every effort to turn the course of the conversation and finally he tired of indirect methods, which hadn't gotten him anywhere. He wrenched the conversation onto the subject he had so obstinately pursued.

"Your dress is very unusual . . . and attractive. Did you get it in Mexico?" His expression dared her to ignore or answer his question with a mere monosyllable.

Raine's eyes crinkled wickedly. "Why, yes, I did. I've just returned from there, as a matter of fact. I traveled rather extensively down there and I also lived for some time in a small village in Baja California."

She could see the next question forming in his eyes. "It was so small it didn't even have a name, but the people were very friendly and I enjoyed my stay with them." She displayed one graceful, tanned arm for his inspection and added, "The swimming and sunbathing were superb," leaving him with the deliberate impression that she had done nothing else for months on end, when in fact she had done some excellent work during that productive period.

"You traveled extensively?" he pursued. Now that he had gotten her talking, he wasn't going to waste the opportunity. "I understand that travel outside of the major urban centers is sometimes difficult. Did you hire a car? And a guide?"

"Oh, I employed a variety of methods of travel." She grinned reminiscently. "The train service was generally adequate to my needs and the buses are fairly reliable if you're not in a hurry to get to your destination." *If you don't mind sharing the accommodations with a variety of protesting livestock at times,* she added silently, and remembering some of the mountain roads, finished mentally, *And if you have a strong set of nerves and a fatalistic outlook on life.* She had even ridden donkeyback and had traveled by what she had later sworn was a prehistoric oxcart.

"I speak Spanish adequately, so a guide wasn't necessary." Her Spanish was of the Castilian variety, but she had a quick ear for languages and had picked up Mexican Spanish easily. Also, although she wouldn't think of telling Nick, her artist's sketchbook was a passport to easy relationships with the people she encountered. Many a poor Mexican family had a Talbot sketch of their offspring, prized for the instinctive recognition of its quality rather than the monetary value, which would have been considerable.

He could see that she was telling him only a fraction of all there was to know but, short of using rack or thumbscrews, he was at a loss to decide how to make her tell him what he really wanted to know. She had answered each question that he had put to her, and still he knew nothing about her, except that she was a master at evasion.

Raine was enjoying his dilemma . . . and he could sense it. Her loquacity was proving to be as obstructive as an outright refusal to answer. She sipped delicately at her cooling coffee, waiting for his next question.

He was of two minds whether to resign the field temporarily, but grim determination made him give it one last shot. Raine was serene. Nick was seething. He was not accustomed to being balked and had no liking for the sensation.

He attacked directly, throwing manners and circumlocution aside. "Did you find it difficult to get a work permit while you were in Mexico? I imagine that with such extensive traveling you found it necessary to supplement your funds from time to time." He had passed beyond the bounds of civility, driven by a frustrated need to find out *something* about the enigmatic woman who had mysteriously attached herself to his mother and then defied him to object.

"I shouldn't have thought that there would be very many jobs in Mexico for itinerant, unskilled labor."

Raine was tremendously diverted. She didn't imagine Nick Hunter had ever had to descend to such depths. "Oh," she drawled, "I found the Mexican officials most helpful wherever I went, but as it turned out, I had no need for a work permit. I had sufficient funds and, of course, one can live very cheaply away from the larger cities if one is willing to adapt the life-style of the general populace. I usually stayed in the Mexican equivalent of the bed-and-breakfast one finds in England and on the Continent. Most are quite clean if somewhat lacking in frills."

Frills certainly hadn't been lacking in the luxury hotels she had patronized periodically when she went to the major cities to ship completed canvases and to renew her supplies. Monterrey, Mexico City, Veracruz, Guadalajara—she had crisscrossed Mexico, painting, touching lives with many.

In Mexico City she had renewed an old family friendship with the American ambassador and had attended a party in honor of several visiting United States senators who were charmed to be allowed to convey personal messages and presents to Raine's families, the Talbots and the Fishers. Raine kept in frequent, if sporadic, contact with her parents and Johnny's and had no compunction about using high-ranking messengers when the opportunity offered itself.

It was hard to tell who might have disgraced him-or herself first, Nick or Mary, had not a dark-suited, hard-faced man appeared suddenly at Nick's elbow with a whispered message, the import of which deepened the scowl already marring Nick's dark face. He stood abruptly and nodded curtly to the hovering minion who disappeared as silently as he had come.

"You ladies will have to excuse me. There seems to be a bit of trouble in the main casino. I will join you in time for Selene's show." He wheeled out in the wake of the man who had come to summon him.

Nick was hardly out of earshot before Mary succumbed to an irresistible fit of laughter. She whooped and snorted into the napkin that she used first to muffle her mirth and finally to mop her streaming eyes. Throughout the display Raine sipped her coffee and maintained a bland facade, with only the slightest tuck at the corner of her mouth to betray her control.

"Oh, Raine, is it wicked of me to laugh so at my son?" Mary gasped when she could speak again. "I've never seen him work so hard and find out so little. He was furious!"

"Wasn't he though?" Raine agreed, with just a tinge of satisfaction. Her provocation had been deliberate, designed to destroy any burgeoning interest Nick Hunter might be developing in her as a possible conquest. Like Selene, Raine hadn't missed the intensity of Nick's scrutiny, and while it was logical to conclude he was motivated by a desire to protect his mother, she had recognized that there was also a certain amount of dangerous, purely masculine speculation in the dark gaze that had assessed her so thoroughly and unremittingly.

Mary folded her napkin and laid it beside her half-empty coffee cup. "Shall we adjourn to the ladies' room before we join Nick? I have a feeling that my mascara is in need of urgent repair. I don't want to appear smudgy."

Raine laid her own napkin aside and said, straight-faced, "But, Mary, I've always been particularly fond of raccoons. They're charming creatures."

"Ooh," Mary groaned theatrically. "That bad? Laughter may be good for the soul, but it plays havoc with eye makeup." She grew serious for a fleeting second and patted Raine's slender hand. "Thank you, Raine. I wasn't sure I'd ever laugh again. You're very good for me."

Mary led the way to their table. Nick was waiting and he stood at their approach. He pulled out a chair for each of them, maneuvering Raine smoothly into the chair next to his own, with Mary on her other side. His hand brushed Raine's shoulder briefly as he tucked the chair beneath her and slid it forward, but it was a butterfly touch, fleeting and swiftly gone. Nothing to make much of, perhaps not even deliberate.

"Did you clear up the trouble, Nick?" Mary asked when he had resumed his own seat.

"Yes. It was just a gentleman who had overextended himself and wasn't happy to be denied further credit. Normally my night manager would handle it himself, but the gentleman knew I was in the hotel and insisted on hearing the decision from me personally." Nick's mouth twisted in a sardonic smile. "He heard it."

Raine could guess what it had been. Nick had been angry when he had left them in the restaurant and she rather imagined that the importunate gentleman had experienced a share of the choler that Nick had been unable to vent on another, perhaps more deserving, head, to wit, her own!

In this she wronged Nick. He had been furious, true, both with her and with himself, but his personal concerns were never allowed to interfere with his business decisions. Selene was a case in point. He had made her his mistress, to be sure. She was attractive and certainly available, but the fact that she had satisfied his physical needs would not have added one day to the length of her contract had she not pleased the customers. Convenience and his own comfort had gained her temporary tenancy of the green suite, but had added not a dollar to the stipulated sum called for in her contract. He might make her occasional gifts when she had pleased him particularly, but they were paid for from his private funds. There were no comminglings of his personal and business affairs on any level.

The gambler had been refused further credit because he was a loud and poor loser, a slow payer, and already overextended to several other casinos in the area. The word was out on him and he had been put on a pay-as-you-go-basis until further notice. Nick had merely made sure that he now had the word.

With a flick of the wrist Nick summoned a waiter. Mary, mindful of her doctor's advice counseling moderation for her comfort's sake, contented herself with a weak Scotch and soda. Nick's startled glance at his mother was noted by Raine but missed by Mary. This was the second time in one day that Mary had acted out of character. She normally downed her Scotch straight from the rocks, and Nick felt the first stirrings of a nebulous disquiet that was to grow in the coming days.

Raine was still engaged in appraising the progress of the vintner's art as represented by the available California vintages and she had a natural preference for wine over hard liquor anyway. She made her selection from the wine list that the waiter had procured at Nick's quiet-voiced request. The half bottle of Cabernet Sauvignon she'd ordered was presented to her with a rather flamboyant flourish by a waiter who should have known better. He uncorked it, poured a sample for her approval, and then filled her glass rather too full. She set it aside for the nonce to allow it to breathe and settled back in her comfortable chair to watch, and enjoy, she hoped, the forthcoming show.

The young comic was entertaining, if still a trifle rough around the edges, and Raine decided that he'd probably be heard from in later years and not just as the lead-in warm-up for the featured performer. He left the audience in a mellow mood and the hum of conversation and clink of glassware obediently died away when the houselights dimmed. The pinpoint of light that was focused on a small, glittering silver circle widened rapidly to reveal a sinuously draped Selene lounging in the curve of her accompanist's grand piano.

A healthy spatter of applause and some encouraging whistles seemed to energize her and she uncoiled from her pose to begin her first song. She sang it directly to Nick, the words and the yearning inclination of her body perfectly suited to her testament of possession. Raine stifled a grin but she was afraid that her table companions could still feel the waves of amusement radiating from her. It was so trite that it was hilarious. She sensed rather than saw Nick shift restlessly beside her and she was sure that she heard a suspiciously muffled snigger from Mary. She hoped that it hadn't carried over to Nick, but she was afraid that it had, because there was a definite, displeased hiss of indrawn breath from the area beside her. She didn't think it came from a lurking waiter.

Judged dispassionately, Selene had a flexible voice that she used well, within its range. Her style and abilities were perfectly suited to the type of singing she was doing now and while Raine couldn't agree with Mary's earlier assessment that she was nothing more than a no-talent cabaret singer, Selene lacked that indefinable, ephemeral something called "star quality." She should, however, do very well for herself in her current niche until her looks begin to fail, or sag, Raine amended as she watched the silver serpent undulate across the stage.

The words of the songs varied, but all had in common a crooning sensuality with which Selene cast forth sticky webs to ensnare the masculine component of the audience. That she had not totally succeeded in enmeshing the one for whom she had tossed the widest and most blatant net became apparent when she joined them at the table at the conclusion of the show.

As Selene approached the table and assessed the seating arrangement, her eyes narrowed coldly. There was room for her beside Nick at the table for four, but that still left Raine at his other side. Selene devised her plan in an instant and, when Nick rose at her approach, she took advantage of the fact that he had moved away from his seat to stand behind the one he had pulled out from the table for her. She dropped deftly into the seat he had vacated and shot a maliciously triumphant glance at Raine.

Nick's scowl, which had appeared in milder form in the restaurant, returned in a thunderous display across his brow. His face looked like the last sight a terrified pioneer might have seen before a war club descended with crushing finality. Raine made a mental note to ask Mary if her late husband had indeed carried Indian blood in his veins. She had never done a portrait out of time but there was something so ruthless and primitive burning in the lean man who watched while Selene took his seat at their table that Raine's fingers itched to have sketching pencils and paper before her.

Raine resolutely refused to glance over at Mary. If Mary had once thought she would never laugh again, she was now permanently disabused of the notion. The triangle of which Raine formed such an unwilling third angle was providing enough laughter for a situation-comedy laugh track!

Neither Nick nor Selene saw the humor of the situation however. Selene's satisfied feline smile froze on her face when she turned back toward Nick. He hadn't taken the chair intended for Selene, but instead still stood, looking down at the two women seated in such close proximity. His expression, as his gaze moved between them, was cruelly contemplative. Selene's face paled beneath its mask of makeup.

Presumably because she still had a late show to do, Selene hadn't removed any of the dramatic stage makeup she had applied with such a lavish hand. The contrast between the two younger women was almost painful. Though they were almost the same age, Selene's ripeness was already overblown, while Raine's maturity transcended flesh and would only mellow richly with additional years.

Without a word Nick reached out and drew Selene to her feet with a hard hand around her upper arm. The band, a versatile and highly professional combo, had begun to play a medley of popular show tunes. Nick guided Selene onto the dance floor with a grip that would have been more suitable for a prisoner being escorted to stand before a judge for sentencing. Once the couple had reached the crowded privacy of the dance floor, the two women who had been so abruptly deserted could see his mouth begin to move in speech. He obviously wasn't whispering intimate nothings in a happily attentive ear! Selene seemed to visibly shrink inside of her tight silver skin. Her expression was stricken and the face she tilted up pleadingly toward the feral implacability of Nick's visage looked suddenly haggard, even in the muted light.

"I rather think Selene has just cooked her opulent goose," was Mary's smug observation. "The one thing Nick will never tolerate from any of his women is possessiveness."

That statement wasn't calculated to inspire a sensation of rejoicing in Raine. If Selene's moon of desire was really on the wane, Nick would inevitably be baying after fresh prey. Raine could hear the chill echo of the *view halloo* floating around her ears. An unfamiliar shiver rippled up her spine.

76

"Mary, I think I've had enough for the evening." Raine had decided that whatever Mary chose to do she was going back to her room right then. She didn't care to be a witness to either the solution or the dissolution of the relationship between Nick and Selene. Perhaps Mary would enjoy having a ringside seat at a massacre, because if it came down to a contest of wills between Nick and his mistress, Raine knew very well who would do the bleeding! But Raine herself had no taste for butchery and Nick hadn't seemed to be in the mood to use anything but the bluntest of blunt instruments.

Also, Raine privately admitted to a measure of culpability. Her continued presence could only exacerbate the situation, because it was obvious to the meanest of intelligence that it had been Raine's advent on the scene that had triggered Selene's possessive reactions. Unwittingly, and certainly unintentionally, Raine had trespassed on territory that Selene had marked as wholly her own. That the territory had objected to being so designated was neither here nor there as far as Raine was concerned.

"Oh." There was a wealth of disappointment packed into that one small syllable. "Must we really go now, Raine? It would be so rude to leave before Nick and Selene return to the table." Mary's attempt to convey an artless sense of propriety was a resounding failure.

"Stay if you like, Madame Defarge. Just try not to get too much blood on your knitting." Raine responded dryly and stood up.

Mary sighed with resignation. Raine was right. It was time for them to go. Her own sense of decency dictated the only course open to them. She didn't like Selene, but humanity required that the woman be allowed to receive her *congé* (and Mary hoped that *that* was what she was going to get!) without any witnesses.

Besides, Mary decided practically, it might save Raine from an unpleasant scene. Selene was going to blame Raine for her downfall even though it was her own behavior that had precipitated her fall from grace. Mary was totally certain that Raine could chew Selene up and spit her out in little pieces if it became necessary, but it would undoubtedly leave a bad taste in Raine's mouth, which might sour the flavor of the relationship Mary still had hopes of seeing develop between this woman, who was already dearer to her than a daughter, and her arrogant, refractory, exasperating, but still beloved, son.

Raine glanced over toward the dance floor while Mary was rising to her feet. At first she didn't see Selene and Nick amid the press of the other dancing couples, but a glint of silver coruscating amid the duller dresses of the other dancers drew her eye. It was hard to interpret the scene, since Nick's head was bent as he listened to the words that poured from the woman he held in his arms and Raine couldn't see the expression on his face, but he was obviously listening. She wouldn't have bet a nickel, plugged or otherwise, on Selene's chances of getting him to do even that much.

Raine felt a small smile curve the corners of her mouth. Selene had just begun to fight and she evidently had some pretty potent weapons still tucked away in her arsenal. The slight smile widened into a grin when she saw Selene's hand creep slyly up from Nick's shoulder to burrow into the straight black thickness of his hair. The lady didn't miss a trick.

Unfortunately for the effect Selene was attempting to create, Nick stopped listening so attentively and looked over at the table where he had left his mother and Raine. He saw them standing, preparing to move away from the table.

Mary was already heading toward the door and Raine was following her when some instinct made her sweep a glance behind one last time. What she saw induced her to quicken her step. With two slightly longer than ladylike strides she caught up with Mary and subtly quickened the pace of their egress as much as she could without actually gripping Mary by the elbow and urging her into a run.

Nick was in pursuit. Or, rather, Raine presumed that's what he was, because he certainly wasn't dancing anymore. He was cleaving a single path through the other dancers on the floor and the scowl was back in place. Raine had had time to see that much in her hasty backward glance and she wasn't taking time to see more. She didn't know whether Nick had actually abandoned Selene on the dance floor and right now she really didn't care.

The only thing Raine knew for sure was that she had no desire to be either a witness to or a participant in another scene with Nicholas Anthony Hunter tonight and would even go to the extent of abandoning Mary, temporarily of course, just for the rest of the evening, to avoid having to parry Nick's persistent thrusts as he sought to pierce the armor of Raine's reserve.

They had gotten as far as the main lobby, halfway to the sanctuary of Raine's room, when the prickling on the back of her neck reached an acute level. From the corner of her eye she could see the somber elegance of a dark, evening-suited figure closing rapidly on them. The only defense was attack.

A touch on Mary's arm and a quiet word stopped their progress and Raine half-turned to confront a long-striding Nick Hunter. Raine had to admit that he had excellent coordination. He didn't crash into them in spite of their abrupt stop, and, while his physical balance hadn't been impaired, Raine didn't allow him the chance to regain his mental equilibrium.

"Ah, Mr. Hunter," Raine purred. "How fortunate. You're just in time to escort your mother to her suite. She was a trifle tired and had decided that she'd had enough . . . excitement . . . for one evening. Since you're here, I'll wander into the casino for a short while." Raine bent forward and kissed Mary's powdered cheek lightly. "I'll see you tomorrow, Mary. Have a good night."

"Good night, Raine, dear," Mary echoed obediently, her eyes twinkling.

Raine bathed all in the vicinity with a dazzling smile and, before another word could be spoken, disappeared. Mary slipped her hand through Nick's unresisting arm and nudged him gently into motion in the direction of her suite.

Raine had no intention of gambling. She slipped into and out of the casino without breaking stride. Another time she would visit it again. Not to gamble, but to observe those who did, and perhaps to record their emotions. Plans for a series of sketches were already taking nebulous form in her subconscious. People were motivated by the common emotions wherever they were—love, hate, greed, hope, despair . . . and fear.

And right now she was motivated by the fear that Nick would intercept her before she reached the privacy of her room. Either Mary had delayed him sufficiently or he had looked for her first in the casino, because she slipped into her room without hail or hindrance. She locked the door behind her and shot the privacy bolt. Even the master key couldn't defeat that barrier and she wouldn't put it past Nick to use his key to allow him access to her room, with or without her permission. There had been a very determined look on his face when she had outmaneuvered him in the lobby. As a final impudent gesture she slipped a DO NOT DISTURB sign over the outer doorknob before she locked the door.

She was washing her face and brushing her teeth when he came. He knocked. The running water masked the sound. The doorknob turned freely, but the privacy bolt held. There was an irritating rattle of the door, much indicative of frustration, and then silence.

Raine's sleep that night was deep and peaceful.

CHAPTER IV

Raine was rudely roused from the restful sleep of one whose conscience is clear by the thin-throated *brrring* of the phone. She was slow to orient herself because she wasn't used to alarm clocks or phones shattering her slumber. Roosters crowing, yes, but they were gentle disturbers of somnolence compared to the shrill mechanical summons that had shocked her awake and upright, heart pounding, amid the tangle of covers.

Her husky "Hello?" reflected both her lingering drowsiness and the dryness of her throat.

"Raine?"

"Yes, Mary." Raine had no clear idea of the time, and anxiety for Mary tinged her questions. "Is anything wrong? Do you need me?"

Mary chuckled. "I gather I woke you up. Do you know what time it is, Raine?"

By that time Raine had managed to scramble for her watch and a squinted examination of its face by the light of the bedside lamp produced an answer, "It's nine o'clock!" in horrified accents. "I haven't slept this late in *years!*"

"The corrupting influence of civilized decadence at work." Mary laughed.

"And a good innerspring mattress," Raine admitted cheerfully. "Have you already eaten breakfast?"

"Not yet. I just got up myself twenty minutes ago," Mary admitted unrepentently. "I thought I'd order breakfast for us both in my suite, unless you'd rather go to the restaurant."

And run the risk of having to break her fast across the table from Nick and/or Selene? Not a chance! "A two-egg Spanish omelet with sausage links as a side order, orange juice, and a pot of coffee, please," Raine dictated hastily. "I'll be with you in fifteen minutes."

Raine glanced at herself in the mirror before she went to join Mary. Even she was tired of her jeans. Today she'd make arrangements to rent a car for the duration of her stay and, if Mary felt up to it, they'd go for a drive after Raine had done some increasingly necessary shopping.

She checked her remaining sheaf of traveler's checks. There were plenty. Although her accommodations often varied from the sublime to the ridiculous, Raine never traveled on a shoestring. Her choice of lodging and mode of travel were dictated by her mood, not by financial necessity. Talbots commanded a price worthy of their quality, but even had they not, her private income, guarded by trusts stemming from both the Talbot and Fisher interests, could have sent her around the world many times over in first-class luxury. Raine regarded the money as a convenience, to be utilized when desirable, but had it not been available, she would still have contrived. The money hadn't saved Johnny. *People* were important. *Things* were dispensable.

"You really put Nick through the hoop last night," Mary observed gleefully.

"Purely unintentional, I assure you." Raine responded uncomfortably and speared a piece of sausage.

"I know. That's what makes it so delightful. Don't get me wrong, Raine. I love my son very much, but he's treated a number of women callously over the years and I can't help but think that you'll be a salutary experience for him, one woman who didn't immediately succumb to his charisma. You probably won't believe it, based on what you've seen of him so far, but he can be devastating when he puts his mind to it." It was Mary's secret hope that Raine would see a sample of Nick's charm, and soon.

"The serpent in Eden was charming," Raine retorted tartly, reading Mary's mind easily. "I'm going to rent a car and then go shopping." She changed the conversation firmly. "Do you want to shop with me? If not, I'll come back for you after I'm done and we'll go for a ride, unless you have other plans already?"

"Oh, I'm sure you could use one of the hotel's company cars, Raine," Mary began impulsively and then finished resignedly. "Well, all right. I suppose that wouldn't be a good idea from your point of view," she said in answer to Raine's emphatically negative headshake.

"The only way I can stay, Mary, is to pay my own way. Remember, though, I can well afford to do so." Raine was not normally so ferociously protective of her independence. Had there been only Mary to consider, she would gracefully have accepted the hospitality offered, but she would accept nothing that ultimately derived from Nick Hunter. She must not give him the slightest ammunition to use against her. She sensed that with all of her deepest instincts, feminine instincts which had long been sleeping, but which Nick Hunter had reawakened with an ease that both surprised and dismayed her. It was an unexpected situation as well as an unwelcome one and, unless she was careful, it might also become an unendurable one!

"I don't believe I'll shop with you, but I would enjoy a ride. I'm ashamed to admit it, but it's been years since I've toured the area. There were so many other things to do . . . and there was always plenty of time . . ." Her voice trailed away and she laid her fork aside, the morsel impaled on its tines untasted, previous bites turned now to ashes and gall in her throat.

"Mary, there is time for every important thing in your life." Raine's calm assurance led Mary away from the engulfing quicksand of depression.

"Tell me until I believe it, please, Raine," Mary begged.

"I will. You will." Raine's quiet pledge offered sure comfort. "Did Nick stay with you long last night?" Raine deliberately turned the conversation to a subject she knew Mary would be unable to resist.

"Not too long," Mary replied. "Especially after he found out that I wouldn't tell him what he wanted to know about you."

"Such as . . . ?"

"Oh, how we had met. Why I had invited you to visit. How long you were staying. And what seemed to concern him most of all, who you were really. Did he come to your room for the answers he couldn't get from me?" Mary was frankly curious.

"Not that I know of," Raine said. "I shot the privacy bolt, just in case, but I didn't hear anything."

They finished breakfast and Raine was careful to keep the topics of conversation light and distracting. They discussed special points of scenic beauty, planned several day-long outings for the days to come, each geared to Mary's reduced store of strength, and trod warily around topics that could quickly engulf them in the morass of Mary's under-standable, and wholly natural, tendency toward self-pity.

Raine left Mary in a cheerful frame of mind and was reasonably certain that it would endure until she had returned from her shopping expedition. Raine stopped by the main reception desk, and using her passport for identification, cashed several traveler's checks which she tore from their book of moderately large denomination. Her clothes purchases could be paid for with more checks, as could the car rental deposit, but she did like to have cash on hand as well.

In spite of her clothes, the reception clerk made no demur about cashing the checks, not even asking whether she was a guest of the hotel. Raine didn't think that he recognized her name though, as he would have, had Nick made mention of her to his staff, because he displayed no outward sign of anything more than helpful courtesy.

Raine would have been amused to know that the

young man had been impressed, not by her physical appearance, but by the well-traveled shabbiness of her passport. He secretly longed to see the exotic corners of the world firsthand and the crowded testament of entry and exit stamps had overawed him, making him momentarily forget an ironclad hotel rule: the privilege of obtaining funds from the reception-desk cashier is extended only to hotel residents.

When the matter came to Nick's attention several days later during a routine review of disciplinary actions, he called the young man to his office, absolved him on the grounds that she was in fact a guest in the hotel, chewed him out for forgetting to ask, and then questioned him closely concerning all he could remember about the incident, specifically any pertinent information gleaned from the passport itself, including some of the more recent of Raine's ports of entry.

The rental car was easily obtained. Raine had a valid American driver's license, renewed periodically, as necessary, during her visits to her family, as well as her international driver's license and the aforementioned passport. And of course they were happy to take her traveler's check.

Raine returned to the hotel in a car well laden with boxes and shopping bags, wearing one of her new purchases, the disreputable jeans having been shoved deeply into one of the bags beneath more stylish garb. She turned the bulk of the packages over to two hovering bellboys and trailed after them, carrying a number of plastic-shrouded dresses over her arm.

It was unfortunate that the procession encountered Nick in the corridor leading to Raine's room. Raine would have been the first to admit that the little procession bore a distinct resemblance to a safari setting out into trackless wastes and having to carry every pot and pan with them, but she failed to see what there was about it otherwise to bring such a glower of displeasure to Nick's face. He didn't keep her in suspense long.

Raine unlocked the door to her room, ushered the burden-bearers inside, and directed them to deposit their loads on the bed. Nick had followed them in without her permission and he took it upon himself to tip the two men and dismiss them without consulting Raine. She busied herself with hanging the dresses draped over her arm up in the closet, until she was sure she once again had her temper under control, and then she faced him warily across the width of the room.

For an almost timeless moment there existed a charged stillness between them that was broken only when Nick took several steps closer to her. Raine didn't retreat physically . . . there was no place else to go, but she immediately raised intangible defensive barriers between them as a counter to the tangible power of his personality. His slow and sensual inspection of the new clothes and the body beneath them brought an angry flush to her cheeks.

He was dressed casually in dark-brown brushed denims and a thin knit short-sleeved sweater of a warm caramel color. With deliberate emphasis he mocked the stance she had assumed—was it only the day before—while she had waited for him to initiate their first confrontation in this very room. He spread his legs slightly for balance and then hooked his thumbs in the belt loops of his jeans, the picture of a man who had all day . . . and possibly all night.

Raine had met many men in the years and the course of her travels since Johnny's death, but never a man like this one. She had met handsome men, charming men, sensual men. She knew men of power and men of sensitivity, but none had moved her to more than academic interest. This man disturbed her. She was aware of a certain ruthless masculinity, elemental and fundamental, that tried to burn through the icy barrier she had unconsciously erected around her deepest emotions and threatened to awaken dormant dragons she had thought long dead. No wonder Selene was so frantic to hold him!

She had not thought to fear him. He was all she despised in a man. He trusted no woman. He used women and discarded them. Mary had said that he could be charming. Raine had seen no evidence of charm, but she could feel the impact of a bone-deep virility that transcended rationality and touched deep, instinctive levels of physical feminine nature.

Raine had known no lover save Johnny. She wanted no other. But there was a fire in this man. It burned uncontrolled, undisciplined, so that his desire blazed brightly for this woman, that woman, but always in time, short or long, burned itself out, leaving cold dead ashes rather than fiery-hearted coals that could flame again and again for the same woman. He was wildfire, untamed and devastating, but if he were to build his fire someday within the hearth of an enduring relationship . . .

"It would seem that you have had a most profitable morning." Nick's voice was cream-smooth, but his eyes flicked derisively toward the tumble of boxes and bags on her bed.

Ahhh, Raine realized with curious relief. *He's jumped to conclusions again.* Before she had met him, she hadn't cared whether or what he thought about her. Now every misconception he nurtured was a form of protection she welcomed. "Profitable to the proprietors of the shops, certainly," she agreed evasively, unwilling to dispel his patent belief that she had taken the opportunity to augment her wardrobe at Mary's expense. *They say. Quhat say they? Let thame say.*

He took another step closer. "Have you come to offer me another bus ticket out of town, Nick?" Raine's expression and tone were glacial.

His smile held no mirth. "That was a mistake," he admitted. "I should never have offered you a bus ticket."

Raine disbelieved her ears. Was he apologizing?

"You're a lady who likes to travel first class," he continued coolly.

Well, that answered her question. He wasn't apologizing!

"Besides, I think I'd like to see you stay around for a while. You're running up a fairly heavy tab, but I'm willing to collect something on account now and then. Who knows? The green suite might become available and I'm sure . . ."

He never finished. Raine covered the rest of the distance between them, moving as quickly and as instinctively as she had when she'd gone to Mary's aid. Her swinging slap across his face echoed sharply in the room.

His reflexes were as swift as her own. She didn't get a chance for a second blow. He grabbed her wrists and immobilized them behind her back with almost contemptuous strength, forcing her lower body against his own by the pressure he exerted against her wrists, pressing them into her spine below the small of her back.

Every ineffectual struggle ground their hips together. Raine ceased her writhing abruptly when she realized that he was enjoying and responding to the stimulation of her captive body as it strained to free itself.

"Fight me some more, little wildcat," he whispered encouragingly and huskily into her ear as she stood rigidly within the unbreakable enclosure of his arms. "Let's melt that ice you try to chill me with. There's fire inside you. I want to warm myself in your flames."

Suggestive, emotive, the dark, rich sound of his voice wove a heated spell in her mind, in its way as seductive as the all-too-human warmth of the lean muscularity of his body. She had been held in a man's arms . . . for comfort. Father, brother, friend. She had accepted the contact of their bodies in a sexless affirmation of wordless concern. They had offered the solace of human touch.

Nick was not offering comfort.

She could not fight, and win, with the handicap of her weaker body. For the first time since he had enclosed her within the prison of his strength she lifted her head to look him in the face. Words could be weapons too.

She had marked him. The darker hue of stung skin spread its stain across the plane of his cheek and a small thread of blood had smeared at the corner of his mouth. While she watched, the tip of his tongue slid out and tasted the wound she had inflicted.

Her eyes traveled higher and clashed with stunning force against the somber desire in his hooded gaze. A mingling of emotions vied for preeminence within those depthless eyes, but desire predominated, and would rule. What she had intuitively dreaded had happened. The magnetic polarity, man to woman, had proved stronger than his aversion to her presumed fortune-hunting persuasions. He knew her price and had decided that she might be worth it!

She parted her lips, desperate now to wield the only weapon left to her—words. "Nick, you . . ."

His seeking, mastering mouth shattered her word-weapons into scintillating shards of pure sensation. She was raped by his kiss. Her parted lips betrayed the path to his invasion and once within her defenses, he plundered the intimate treasures at will.

She tried to jerk her head away. One hand moved up from her wrists to the back of her neck, imprisoning her head in a remorseless, inescapable grip, entwined tightly in the gold silk of her hair. She twisted, she struggled, desperate to escape. She tasted blood . . . his? Hers? Her mouth ached from the savage pressure, and yet softened and yielded beneath the demand for submission.

No kindly deus ex machina intervened. No phone call, no urgent knock at the door of her room interrupted at the critical moment. She was defeated, malleable to his overwhelming demands and he sensed her inability to escape. She sagged limply against his arms and the lax surrender of her suddenly pliant body misled him. He eased his hold on her wrists, intending to take advantage of her submission to fill his hand with the rich swell of her breast. She would fit and overflow the cup of his palm and the taut thrust of her nipple would tease them both toward fulfillment.

He felt moisture on his cheeks and tasted the brine of tears mingling with the salt tang of blood from the inner surfaces of their mouths. He freed her captive lips from the demand and domination of his own, lifting his head away. Her eyes were closed and tears welled through wet, spiky lashes to slide in slow procession down her smooth cheeks. He stepped back, a half step, no more. Her arms hung limply at her sides, neither holding nor thrusting him away and her head remained tilted back, blind still to the fact that he no longer compelled her by his superior strength. His hands slid up from her wrists and around from the back of her neck to rest with fingertip pressure on her shoulders. He shook her slightly. She swayed, a slender sapling in the wind, but still those slow, sad tears slipped down from some inner, overrunning source.

"Raine!" His voice commanded.

Obediently her weighted lids lifted. He looked down into blue eyes whose pupils had expanded into lightless lakes, reflecting a silent shriek of pain so unbearable that it reverberated in his mind louder than a scream of mortal anguish.

"You had no right!" Her choked whisper condemned him. "I am not *yours*. You soil me to use me as you would your women. You are not Johnny. I am not Selene. Go to her to sate your lust! I am no fouled well where you may slake your thirst."

Each lethal word was a tiny cat-o'-nine-tails, flaying with stinging, deliberately placed lashes. If words were to be her only weapon, she would make sure that she needed no others. His face drained of color, leaving it ashen. Without a word he left her. She stood alone in the empty room, arms wrapped tightly around her waist in an attempt to ease some unremitting pain, and the slow tears streamed down her cheeks again.

Later, when she was calmer, she remembered her words and was appalled. She had attacked viciously, meaning to slash and wound. Nothing that Nick had done to her could justify the things that she had said to him. He had insulted her. He believed her to be scheming and mercenary and . . . he had kissed her. Brutally, punitively, he had ravaged her mouth, but . . .

She tallied the list. The insult? The slap had paid that debt. That he had such a low opinion of her morals and character? She had laughed at that misreading of her character and even now it stirred her more to mirth than to ire. But the kiss? There lay the crux of the matter!

That kiss had caused her such wrenching mental torment that she had, in a wild frantic defense, struck out in a futile attempt to ease her own agony by causing Nick equal or worse pain. And that had been

95

wrong, terribly, dreadfully wrong. Nick's passionate, possessive kiss had been the first man's kiss given or taken since Johnny's last tender salute. Nick had taken something that had belonged to Johnny only and, at that moment, she had hated him, and had punished him, for being alive while Johnny was dead.

She could not yet bear to consider the implications of what she had just admitted to herself, but one thing was clear. She would have to apologize to Nick. She owed him that. Nick's crime had been committed against a memory and his punishment had been excessive.

But not today. She couldn't face him again today . . . and remember. Tomorrow would be soon enough. Tomorrow she would go to him and make her apologies. And explanations? No. She deeply regretted all that had happened, and regretted her loss of control most of all, but it entitled Nick to no explanations. She wouldn't take him on a walk through her mind and memories. She owed him courtesy. She didn't owe him confession.

Raine's anomalous defensiveness where Nick was concerned should have served as *caveat*. Her initial insouciance, before and after she had met him, had not prepared her for the devastation he would wreak on her emotions and her previous ability to calmly order the direction of her life.

Mary knew her son. She had seen him grow up, had seen the man he had become and her actions had helped to shape him. Raine knew him before she had ever set eyes upon him. Her artist's eye and her own personal prejudices had added to the composite she had drawn of him in her mind, but Nick was more than the sum of her knowledge of him. He was a man. He was flesh and blood, he was human, and he possessed a charisma that words could not convey. He was not merely a composite of opinions: Mary's opinion, Raine's opinion, Selene's opinion. He was himself. And Raine had painfully discovered that he would not fit into the mold she had poured for him.

Nor did she.

For long years she had been a partial person. When Johnny had died she had closed many doors. Gradually she had reopened all but one. Nick had not opened the door she had kept locked and bolted. He had smashed it down.

When she had wept herself empty, Raine went into the bathroom and bathed her tear-marked face in cooling and calming water. Her eyes were swollen and fever-hot from the scalding tears she had shed, and she pressed a thirsty terry washcloth against the closed lids to soothe the puffiness and redness.

At last she considered that her outward appearance would pass public scrutiny . . . namely Mary's. She possessed no makeup she could use for camouflage and for the first time in a long time she regretted that she had dispensed with the feminine artifices with such completeness! She could have done with some blusher to add color to her cheeks and some foundation concealment to disguise the darkness beneath her eyes. Who would have expected that her excesses of emotion could so mark her face? Who would have expected that she would have to endure such excesses of emotion . . . ?

Mary's voice was unexpectedly normal when

Raine contacted her on the phone. *But why shouldn't it be?* Raine chided herself almost crossly. Mary could have no idea what had transpired between her friend and her son such a short time ago! And Raine wasn't going to tell her either! It would distress her or encourage her and Raine couldn't decide which contingency she wanted to avoid more.

"I've given the local mercantile economy a healthy boost on this month's balance sheets, Mary, and as soon as I've hung up a few more things, I'll be ready to go for our drive." Raine was pleased to note that even to her own critical ear her voice sounded casual and natural. "While I was shopping I heard about an excellent restaurant in Stateline and I thought, since I'd planned to drive down in that direction, that we might like to try it rather than come all the way back to the hotel for dinner. How does that sound to you?" Raine hoped that Mary would agree without further persuasion because there was no way that they were going to sit down for dinner across from Nick tonight, not while Raine still had breath in her body!

"Coward," Mary laughed into the phone. Raine's heart lurched. Mary couldn't know! Nick wouldn't have told her! Then Mary added, "You just don't want to ruin your appetite by having to listen to Selene sing for her supper."

Oh, Selene . . . Raine had forgotten all about her, but she'd make as good a red herring as any. "Well, actually," Raine agreed mendaciously, "I would just as soon not have to listen to Selene again for a while, on or off stage, but if you'd rather come back . . ." She allowed her voice to trail away.

98

"Me neither!" Mary agreed hastily with a sad lack of grammar. "I never wanted to listen to Selene." The discussion was concluded with both parties in perfect agreement, though for widely differing reasons.

While she finished arranging her morning's purchases before she went to pick up Mary, Raine lectured herself sternly. She must not look for hidden meanings in every chance comment Mary made. Nick was not a man who would discuss his private affairs with anyone, especially his mother. If she persisted in starting at nonexistent shadows of meanings, she would soon alert Mary to the situation developing between Nick and herself. *The guilty flee where no man pursueth,* Raine paraphrased silently. And as little as Raine wanted to admit it, a situation was developing and thus far she had seemed unable to halt it or even slow its pace, no matter what strategy she employed. She obviously could not control Nick and she had even begun to fear that she might not be able to retain control of herself. On any scale of measurement Nick had won their last encounter hands down, because her panicky utilization of below-the-belt tactics could not be termed even a moral victory.

Even before they had met, Raine had somehow sensed that it might be necessary to confound and mystify Nick, to shake him off balance, so that she might continue to preserve her carefully guarded privacy. She had managed to retain an upper hand during their first day of sparring, as they had commenced sparring from the moment Nick's eyes had swept across her at the airport. But by the second day

Nick had regained his lost leverage. Now Raine was inexorably being forced into a defensive position. Tomorrow she would have to seek him out to apologize, a prospect she found increasingly daunting and distasteful.

The drive and the dinner were both successful from Raine's point of view. They didn't stay to see the after-dinner show since Mary's reserves of energy were easily depleted, but when Mary invited Raine into her suite to share a post-prandial drink, Raine accepted without a second thought. The purpose behind this visit was to provide them with opportunities to talk, and what better time to begin than now? If the situation between Nick and herself became intolerable, she might have to leave and she wanted to do as much for Mary as she could, just in case.

The bar in the suite supplied the drinks, a weak Scotch for Mary and a small glass of wine for Raine, and they arranged themselves comfortably, Raine in a large armchair and Mary half reclining against the mounded pillows of the couch. They sipped meditatively on their individual drinks as the room's hush grew increasingly portentous. At first Raine had decided that it might be best to allow Mary to approach the subject in her own time and in her own way.

Mary shifted restlessly. She had desperately wanted this opportunity to talk to Raine, but when the time came, her courage failed. How could she ask Raine to rip apart the old, healed scars, to delve among the painful memories, seeking some balm for another's aching wounds?

Raine sensed Mary's reluctance and easily divined its source. She was touched by this evidence of the older woman's sensitivity, but she had already decided she would pay the price to purchase peace of mind for Mary. "Mary," she asked quietly, "may I tell you about Johnny?"

"Please." The single whispered word was starkly poignant.

Raine's voice was low but perfectly clear and controlled. "We fought it. The Fishers and the Talbots have money and connections. Johnny and I went from doctor to doctor, from clinic to clinic. I could not believe that there would not be a miracle for us, that our love could not be strong enough to heal Johnny's rebellious body. But everywhere we went the verdict was the same and the time we were given ticked away, day by remorseless day, even though we tried to hold back the hours in each other's arms. I never knew a night could have such few hours. Sometimes it seemed as though the sun and moon raced each other across the sky."

The cool wine ran down Raine's dry throat, moistening the parched passage. "We spent nearly a year chasing the chimera of a cure. And then, one night, as I cried in his arms, Johnny told me that he'd come to a decision. We had spent our time being preoccupied with death. It was time for us to become occupied with life. If word came of some new, radical discovery in the treatment of illnesses of his type, we would of course pursue it, but otherwise, except for the palliative measures which would eventually become necessary as his illness progressed, he . . . we were finished with the hospitals and the clinics and the doctors who could only say, 'I'm sorry, but perhaps if we try *this* combination of medicines

. . .' But this combination or that combination—none worked."

It seemed easier now. She was reliving the good memories and her words flowed freely. "Johnny wanted to bind himself to life, to draw strength from the things that have endured past man's short span, the things, natural and manmade, that transcend the finiteness of one man's existence and tie all men together in a long chain of shared experience, stretching forward and backward in time. He was looking for his place in the universe.

"When he felt well enough we traveled. We visited the things man has made that spanned the generations. We knelt in cathedrals; we walked in houses that had sheltered people whose bodies were now not even mounds of dust. We touched the chisel marks on the stones of the pyramids. Great paintings, great music—we steeped ourselves in the spirit of humanity to remind ourselves of man's significance, and yet his inconsequence in the scheme of the cosmos. *We* are not expected to order the working of the universe, you know. We also searched out the marvels of nature which far surpass the works of man. We went to an observatory and viewed the dance of nebulae. We felt our bones vibrate from the thundering power of Niagara Falls. We marveled at the relentless geologic persistence that had carved the Grand Canyon. Johnny and I both drew strength from these things.

"There were good days, but not all days were good. Thank God there was not much pain, but there was a steadily increasing lassitude, a gradual dimming of contact with the world. Johnny battled, and so did I, loving him, giving him what strength I could. We won another year, but finally he was so tired and so I let him go *because* I loved him. I would not hold him to a body that had become only a burden to his spirit."

Raine's hands rose and fell back into her lap in a broken gesture of completion, but her face was serene. There was a small, achingly sweet smile curving her mouth and her eyes were tender with love.

"Oh, Raine," Mary whispered painfully. "How did you bear it? Did you not want to . . . to . . . ?"

"To follow him?" Raine finished for her. "Oh, yes, the temptation was there, but how could I have faced him then? It was *his* time. He had completed the purpose of his life. It was not yet *my* time and I would have made a mockery of all we had learned in those years we had together had I set foot on the path which it was not yet my time to tread. Our paths divided for a space, but when it is time they will join again." There was the ring of absolute conviction in her voice.

Mary's voice was urgent. "You really believe that Johnny . . . that you'll be with him again?"

"Oh, yes, Mary. I'm not what the world calls conventionally religious, but that I do know."

They talked for a while longer, and then gradually Raine guided the conversation onto more casual subjects. Mary needed time to ponder and to absorb. When she was ready, she would ask again and Raine would do her best to answer what was inherently an unanswerable question. In the final analysis Mary would have to find her own answers from within herself, but Raine could point out some guideposts which she and Johnny had passed together along that stony path.

When Raine went to her room later that evening the hour was still relatively early, but she was exhausted, wearied by the emotional strain rather than by any physical exertion. She stepped beneath a swift and stinging, hot then cold, shower, but it only served to increase her lassitude. She completed the automatic nighttime rituals with dispatch and within half an hour from the time she had unlocked her door, Raine dropped into the firm embrace of the superior mattress and surrendered to the cool clasp of the fresh sheets.

Tired though she was, sleep would not come, although she wooed it assiduously with a dark room and closed eyes. Her mind spun restlessly with thoughts of the Hunters, mother and son. To block out unwelcome thoughts of the son, she opened the door to the memory of Mary's voice as it had asked, "Do you think that Johnny would mind if you loved and married again?"

Raine had masked, she hoped, the shaft of pain that tore through her like a burning spear, but when she tried to answer, she found, to her surprise, that the words came freely. "No." She had responded slowly, with more than a tinge of wonder in her voice. "He loved me. He would *want* me to find happiness again, as I would want that for him, were the positions reversed. Another love, a new love would not take away from what we had. Love isn't wasted, nor is it selfish, if it is the kind of love Johnny and I had."

They had not spoken of it again, but now, as she lay in bed in the cool dark, Raine's thoughts worried and probed at the subject because it wasn't one she had allowed herself to examine in depth before. Neither her parents nor Johnny's had raised the question, both because they respected her privacy and because they were daunted by the impenetrable barrier of reserve that arose whenever they sought to broach the subject. Mary had felt no such qualms, and now Raine was at last face-to-face with an issue she had avoided since Johnny's death.

With remorseless honesty, Raine examined the topic and the answer. Johnny was not the barrier, and yet, in a strange way, he was. He had been such a special person, so much a part of her life from childhood on that the thought of another standing in the place he had stood had been unthinkable. No man would stand in Johnny's place, but could another man make his *own* place in her life? She had allowed no man to do so, but might there come a time, and a man, who would give her no choice? She shivered, premonition stroking its fingers up the line of her spine.

"No!"

The impulsive negative cracked sharply in the dark room, but the muffling blackness threw back no echoes.

CHAPTER V

It would have taken more than one restless night to erode appreciably Raine's innate vitality, but it was obvious that her sleep had not refreshed her. Painful memories and future apprehensions had combined to cause her to surface and sink continually, in a wearying cycle, in the shallow seas of an unrefreshing slumber. Resolution and discipline would deal with this morning's lethargy, but Raine knew that too many nights like the one she had just gone through would soon show on her face as well as in her spirit.

She admitted it bleakly. She didn't want to face Nick this morning . . . or *any* morning. The temptation to cry craven was insidious and appealing, and so unlike her.

She dragged herself up out of the crumpled tangle of sheets. The maid would remove the evidence of her restless night, replacing it with another crisp, white tablet on which Raine could write her next night's dreams and dreads. But what would wipe away the memory of the look on Nick's face when she had slashed at him viciously with her scathing and scarifying words? Some lacerations go deeper than even the anodyne of an apology can reach, no matter how sincerely and repentently it is tendered.

Well, she reminded herself wryly, *at least I don't have to face him on an empty stomach or even over breakfast.* She and Mary had arranged to eat their breakfast in Mary's suite again this morning. It had been Mary's own suggestion, completely unprompted by Raine, and Raine's slightly suspicious stare had elicited in response only a gaze of utmost innocence from Mary.

As is the way with most women who have an unpleasant interview to face, Raine prepared herself, girded herself, with all the feminine armor she could summon to her aid. Had she been braving Nick's den, hoping to attract him, she would have chosen clothes that pointed up her femininity and hinted at a sensuality, controlled but latent below a thin surface.

But she did not want to attract him, only to apologize to him. Her image was cool, controlled, and composed. The cut and tailoring of her pale blue denim skirt and weskit, the crisp, casual formality of her short-sleeved white and blue striped cotton shirt, and the twisted white leather of her elegantly simple and comfortable low-heeled sandals perfected the image of a woman who is calmly sure of herself, even when performing a personally unwelcome but necessary task. Raine had brushed her hair until the roots tingled from the ruthless bristles of her hairbrush, and the silken gloss of her thick mane shone with rippling lights and highlights as it curved and draped around the shape of her head, covering her ears except for the small, delicate lobes, and twisted into an endlessly repeating coil in the shape of a flattened figure eight—the stylized, mathematical symbol for infinity—at the back of her head.

Raine completed her preparations with a thorough application of a complementary perfume that exactly expressed and summed up the image she wished to project. It was a subtle floral fragrance. She had never favored a heavy perfume, instinctively understanding that subtlety suited and defined her personality because she was not an obvious person. In truth, her waters ran painfully deep. There was, however, a touch of sharp lemon astringency underlying the delicate yet ripening fragrance of blossoms which must one day mature into the rich harvest of luscious fruit. The lemon tartness was an elusive yet explicit warning, mostly subconscious, that an unwary bite could cause the mouth to pucker and that caution was advisable. Raine's choice of the perfume was instinctive. She did not herself understand all the ramifications of the message her selection of fragrance carried.

When she was ready she evaluated herself in the mirror, much as she had done on that first night, and as she had been on that night, she was pleased with the image she saw reflected, not out of vanity, but because it assured her that she had achieved her purpose. In these two instances she felt almost as though she had donned a costume, one which was to be an aid in emphasizing and portraying a character she wished to delineate to an audience. She didn't allow herself to dwell on the fact that in both cases she was basically playing to an audience of one.

Clothes were neither an avocation nor an engrossing interest for Raine, yet she possessed an inborn sense of color and style and a flair for choosing and wearing the correct clothes for the occasion. Her clothes might not always be conventional, but when she wore them, they became what the situation required. Raine did not follow fashion. She made it, but on such a personal basis that another woman could not hope to copy her with an equal degree of success.

Mary seemed in good spirits over breakfast. She had obviously spent a restful night, Raine observed silently and slightly enviously. The awkward moment came after the meal was finished, when Mary inquired about Raine's plans for the morning. Then she unwittingly rescued Raine from the uncomfortable necessity of admitting to an intention to seek an interview with Nick and *that* admission would really have given Mary food for fantasy! Raine wouldn't have wanted to give the real reason she had to speak with Nick and Mary's imagination would have filled in easily, if not accurately.

Mary had an appointment to get her hair done. Raine approved the idea of a prospective shorter and more casual cut as well as the idea of a body wave to lend manageability. She would probably have endorsed anything short of a Mohawk if it kept Mary occupied for long enough, and of course Raine knew all too well the value of the little morale-building exercise.

In answer to Mary's query about Raine's plans for the morning, Raine murmured, "Oh, I'll find something to do. Perhaps I'll sketch or something . . ." and allowed the subject to trail away vaguely.

Raine took the precaution of walking with Mary to the hairdressing salon, which was located within the hotel, and of chatting with her until she had been met and led toward the shampooing section by a smiling young woman. Only then did Raine make her way to the area of the hotel where Mary had previously indicated that Nick had his offices.

Nick's secretary was a surprise. She was neither young nor attractive, but judging by the rattling speed with which her fingers raced upon the keyboard of the typewriter, she was efficient. Nick evidently didn't require glamor in all aspects of his life.

"May I help you?" The question was accompanied by a pleasant smile.

"I would like to speak to Mr. Hunter for a few moments, please. My name is Mrs. Fisher, Raine Fisher." Raine made her request courteously.

The hotel's grapevine must have been abysmal because no flicker of recognition crossed the face of the secretary. "I'm sorry." She tempered her refusal with a sympathetic smile. "Mr. Hunter sees no one without prior appointment and frankly—" humanity unexpectedly broke through when she grimaced slightly "—he hasn't been in a mood to see anyone for several days. If you'd care to give me an idea of the nature of your business with Mr. Hunter, perhaps I could arrange an appointment with him." She didn't sound hopeful. Nick had been very unapproachable, but she sat poised with pad and pencil, ready to record Raine's address, phone number, and

111

the reason why Nick should see her when he was seeing no one else.

"I don't think that will be necessary," Raine replied gently. "Please tell Mr. Hunter that I'm here. I think he'll see me now, without an appointment."

Mrs. Bolt, for that was her name, was well familiar with this particular ploy, and with the women who had used it before, and undoubtedly would again, in an attempt to circumvent her guardianship of Nick's privacy. And yet this woman was different from the others who had stood before her desk demanding admission, demanding Nicholas Hunter's attention, attention he had perhaps given for a while but had since withdrawn. Although their faces and figures had differed and they had been variously blond, brunette, or redhead—Nick's taste was quite catholic—there had been a signature sameness to them all. Indeed this woman was different.

"I don't think . . ." she began doubtfully, more than halfway to a refusal. Nick had been explicit and his "No appointments this morning, Mrs. Bolt" had meant no appointments, Mrs. Bolt, or else! "I really can't . . ." She tried again. It was amazingly hard to refuse the poised young woman who seemed prepared to outface and outwait her for as long as was necessary.

"He will, you know," Raine promised quietly. He would, Raine knew, although she might wish he wouldn't, but she had come to apologize and in spite of her misgivings, that was what she was going to do. Mrs. Bolt was no match for Raine's quiet inflexibility.

"I'll ask him." Mrs. Bolt surrendered with a sigh,

and stood up behind her desk. She wouldn't use the intercom. If she was going to have her head handed to her in a basket, she preferred for it to be done in private. The penalty for miscalculation, if she had miscalculated, would be a tongue lashing at the very least. Nick had been in a very bad mood this morning.

She marched into the inner office, head up, shoulders back, after the briefest of taps on the door.

Nick looked up from his brooding inspection of a sheaf of papers spread over his otherwise orderly desk. He had expected to see Mrs. Bolt, but to see her holding letters for him to sign, not to see her standing emptyhanded and apprehensive, her back against the door. She was clearly uncomfortable but resolute, as though she might be about to perform an act that was risky but necessary. He lifted an interrogatory eyebrow.

"There's a Mrs. Fisher outside. She wants to see you." The words blurted out starkly and the hapless woman braced herself for his reaction.

A complicated expression moved the muscles of Nick's face briefly but she couldn't interpret its meaning. He said, "Raine Fisher," but it wasn't a question and she couldn't decipher his tone of voice any more than she had been able to read the emotions that had flashed across his face. He said only, "Show her in. No calls, Mrs. Bolt."

There was no emphasis in the cadence of his even voice, but Mrs. Bolt got the message. She had gambled when she had listened to her intuition, and she had won, but while the mysterious Mrs. Fisher was in the office, there would be no calls, and no interruptions.

Raine watched Mrs. Bolt reenter the office. The secretary's expression was an almost comical mixture of relief and curiosity, although the relief predominated. Raine didn't need to be a mindreader. It was easy for her to visualize the scene as it must have happened. What she could not visualize or anticipate, however, was the scene that was going to ensue once she had passed through the door that Mrs. Bolt so politely held open for her. She gathered her courage in both hands, smiled slightly at Mrs. Bolt by way of thanks, and went in. Mrs. Bolt closed the door behind her.

Nick was standing behind his desk. In the stern formality of his dark, three-piece suit, he looked anything but approachable. An inscrutability had wiped his face clear of all expression. He didn't even look wary. Raine suddenly understood the phrase *her heart sank*. She could now testify that it was an actual physical sensation. He wasn't going to help her and, after all, there wasn't any reason why he should.

His hand made a restrained gesture, indicating a comfortable-looking, straight-backed chair pulled up beside his desk, wordlessly inviting her to be seated, but he didn't speak or make any other movement. Raine knew he'd thoroughly assessed her appearance, and that even her perfume had been evaluated, because she'd seen his nostrils flare once, twice, as she'd neared him. It was a reaction reminiscent of a many-antlered buck she'd once seen, testing the air for the scent of mate or foe.

She didn't sit down. This wouldn't take long and she wouldn't put it past Nick not to take his own seat after she had subsided meekly into the indicated chair. He might just decide to loom over her, putting her at both a physical and psychological disadvantage.

"I owe you an apology," Raine said stiffly into the charged silence. "I've come to make it." It hardly sounded gracious, but she couldn't help herself. This was even more difficult than she had feared it would be.

She had finally decided that he wasn't going to respond at all and had opened her lips slightly to continue, to get it over with and leave, when his voice cut across her intended speech.

"Sit down, Raine."

She sat automatically, and then was surprised to find that she had done so. Nick's deep voice had exerted such compelling authority that she had obeyed with her body before her mind had had a chance to object.

Her hunch proved accurate. He didn't resume his seat behind the desk. Instead he shoved some papers out of the way and half sat on the edge of the desk nearest to her, uncomfortably close, invading her own personal space. He stared down at her upturned face almost as though he were searching for something, but his own face revealed nothing—not his thoughts, not his feelings.

Raine had mentally rehearsed several speeches of apology. They all fled without leaving the trace of a prepared phrase behind. *Soit.* So be it. Her apology would be extemporaneous and brief, and the sooner she made it, the sooner she could leave Nick's disturbing presence.

With intense effort she kept her hands relaxed, loosely clasped in her lap, while she met his eyes fairly. "Nick, I'm truly sorry for the way I spoke to you, for what I said to you in my room yesterday. You didn't deserve such vilification and I'm ashamed of my loss of control." Her voice stumbled from its clear cadences into a forced whisper. "I was punishing you for something that was not your fault. It will not happen again. Please accept my apologies." It was as much of an explanation as he would get from her, but her regret for the incident was sincere.

Raine could no longer force herself to meet those darkly perceptive eyes. She dropped her gaze to the hands that rested in her lap, waiting for his reaction, any reaction. She could feel his somber stare boring into the top of her bent head. He allowed the silence between them to stretch until she thought she would scream. Then he murmured dangerously, "Prettily spoken, Raine, with just the proper amount of penitence." His rich baritone voice vibrated with an almost rumbling purr, soft, almost menacing in its very evenness. "It lacks, however, something." His tone became almost meditative. "An element of explanation perhaps?" He toyed with her, pressing for a response, using his voice and his physical nearness to coerce her into making an unguarded rejoinder.

"I've said I'm sorry." Raine was compelled to retaliate, however feebly. "I owed you an apology. I've given it." She knew she sounded childish, almost sulky, but she couldn't help herself. He was too close. He loomed above her and she felt stifled, surrounded

116

by the pressure of his mute demand. She would not explain further, not to him!

It was an unfortunate choice of words and Nick took immediate advantage of her unguarded phrasing. "Owe? Oh, yes, Raine Fisher, you owe me several things, and an apology is just one of them." The tone of his voice was one of cool amusement, almost taunting, but she could not mistake his determination to collect, in full, everything he felt she "owed" him.

Raine stiffened angrily. He was impossible, but she had salved her own conscience. She had made her apology, whether he chose to accept it or not. She didn't owe him anything else. She forgot the unsettling effect his physical nearness seemed to have on her heartbeat and breathing. The only thing she felt at the moment was righteous indignation until he spoke again and threw her off balance once more.

"I owe you an apology as well, Raine."

It was the last thing she had expected to hear from him. "An apology? To me?" she repeated blankly, unable to credit her own hearing.

"Yes, an apology. To you." Now his voice was serious, all amusement eradicated. Raine risked a glance upward, careful not to become entangled in the magnetic depths of his dark eyes, but her flickering inspection of his face revealed only sincerity. He *was* going to apologize. For what? Her glance slid away, back down to contemplate her hands.

"Look at me, Raine. I won't apologize to the top of your head." Nick's long-fingered hand, with its short clipped nails and broad palm—it reminded her of the hands of Michelangelo's David, graceful yet

117

embodying masculine strength—came into her field of vision and rested warmly beneath her chin to tilt her head up. It withdrew when her head was positioned as he wished. He had no need to hold her physically. His eyes commanded her attention.

"That's better. Now, my apology." He hesitated and then continued quietly. "Yesterday, in your room, I frightened you . . . hurt you somehow . . . and you cried. I'm sorry. I was angry, but it was never my intention to hurt you. For that I apologize."

Now it was his turn to wait for her reaction. Raine swallowed once to be sure that her voice wouldn't crack and betray her before she managed to say, "I suggest that we call it a draw, Nick. It was a regrettable incident, best forgotten all around. I shan't refer to it again and I'll consider the incident closed."

Raine hoped that she could indeed call the incident closed and she would certainly do her best to ensure that there was no repetition! She felt like a kite on a string, jerked this way and that way by the winds of change that swirled around her. She hadn't been in control of herself or the interview from the moment she had walked into Nick's office. It was time to walk out. She stood up, intending to do just that, but Nick moved to block her, the masculine solidity of his strong body forming a barrier she found impossible to circumvent. If she was determined to leave the office, she would have to go through him.

"Sit down again, Raine," he ordered softly. He was so close that she could feel the warmth of his breath fanning across her brow. "We haven't finished discussing the things you owe me." His voice was steel-threaded silk and he meant to be obeyed.

Mary had assured Raine that Nick had charm, although she hadn't also warned that he was a master in the techniques of intimidation, but then, of course, Mary wouldn't know about that side of him. Raine relaxed in her chair. Nick Hunter might think that he held the winning hand, but he was about to discover that Raine had drawn four of a kind.

She wasn't some impressionable, insipid young virgin, to be overwhelmed and overcome by the practiced virility of an attractive man. Her cards were all aces. She wasn't betting on a busted flush!

On the well-tested principle that attack is the best form of defense, Raine took the fight to Nick. She lounged back in her chair, a feat in itself in a straight-backed chair, rested her elbows on the padded leather arms, and steepled her fingers together in an arch over her lap. With all of her regained poise on show, she arched a curved, slim eyebrow at a slightly disconcerted Nick and drawled with obviously weary patience, "All right, Nick, let's get it over with. Just what do you feel I owe you? Present your bill and we'll square accounts here and now."

"The lady believes in plain speaking." Nick matched her drawl.

"The lady is tired of playing games," Raine responded. "Present your markers, Nick, and I'll show you the color of my money."

"Why are you here?" He accepted her challenge readily.

Raine was tempted to willfully misunderstand him, but she heroically restrained herself. It wouldn't help the situation. He wasn't asking why she had come to his office. They'd already covered that ground! He was addressing the broader issue.

"Nick, I'm here because Mary asked me to come, for no other reason. Someday, soon, I hope, you'll understand why it is important that I stay with her for a while, but I can't—*can't,* not won't—tell you anything more right now. This is Mary's private business and I am not free to discuss it with anyone until she gives me leave to do so. I can only offer you my assurances that I mean her only good and I'm not after any money or financial gain from the situation. I told you before. I pay my own way. My visit with Mary has cost neither her nor you a penny, nor will it."

Raine risked a slight grin at Nick, who had leaned against his desk once more, his arms crossed over his chest as he listened to her. "In spite of what your initial impression of me might have led you to believe, I am eminently respectable and my mode of dress at the time was by choice, not by necessity. My current attire—" she waved a hand down her body "—hasn't cost you or Mary a penny, nor will it in the future."

Her smile faded away and she finished seriously, "Nick, for your sake, and ultimately, for Mary's, you must believe me. I will do her only good."

Nick regarded her silently for a long moment. Raine returned his look calmly. On this ground she had the advantage, her position was impregnable, and he could sense it. There were no chinks in her armor where Mary was concerned and he could hear the truth ringing in every word she had spoken.

He shifted to another area where she might prove vulnerable. "I'll accept your assurances about Mary, for the moment," he promised smoothly, "but if I'm to accept that you pay your own way, I'd like to know how? To be blunt, my dear, you have no visible means of support. You can't blame me for being a trifle . . . ah . . . doubtful about your claims to solvency."

Raine chose not to be offended. She and Nick would always be bare-knuckled opponents, she suspected, and she had only herself to blame. Besides, it was easy to be amused when she knew just how solvent she really was! "Let's just say I'm one of the eccentric independently wealthy. My credit's good, Nick, and if you're worried about my possible depredations in your casino, don't be. I don't gamble, not even on sure things. It's not my bag, and even if it were, I pay as I play. I don't play on credit, neither my own nor on another's."

"You seem to have an answer for everything," Nick jibed deliberately, "but I've yet to see the color of your money."

"Fair enough," Raine responded mildly. From her flat white leather shoulder bag, which had swung at her side throughout the potentially explosive interview, she pulled a thick wad of traveler's check folders and fanned them with a practiced gesture, so that Nick could see the signature in the upper left-hand corner: Raine T. Fisher. His eyebrows rose, both at the thickness of the stack and the denominations of the individual checks.

She couldn't resist. "Is the color good, Nick?" she

purred with sugary innocence. Raine was only human. She could give into her baser instincts as regretably as the next person and she succumbed to the temptation to take a cheap shot.

"You don't mind kicking a man when he's down, do you, Raine?" Nick grinned.

"Just a little object lesson. Snap judgments can be dangerous to the ego, Nick." She twisted the knife a little more. "Yours, not mine," she finished sweetly.

"Whew! You twist a mean knife." His smile widened warmly and his deep chuckle was rueful. Raine felt a queer, breathless sensation clutch at the pit of her stomach. Mary was right. Nick had charm and, most disarmingly, it seemed that he could laugh at himself. Against her better judgment, she smiled back.

Her better judgment was promptly proved to be a shrewd judge of character. While the smile was still curving over her lips, Nick proceeded to wipe it away with his next words.

"I know you're not Selene, Raine. And I am not Johnny. Who is Johnny?" He slid the question between her ribs so smoothly that it took a moment for the jagged edge of the wound to transmit the painful message to her stunned brain.

The color drained from her face . . . she could feel it go . . . and the accompanying weakness caused her to close her eyes briefly. Damn. She'd dropped her guard. She'd been momentarily disarmed by the sorcery of his smile, distracted by the practiced sleight-of-hand that drew the attention away from the critical moment until the riposte could pierce the weakened defense, straight to the vulnerable heart.

Her answer was spoken in a clear monotone. "Johnny was my husband. Johnny is dead." She rose to her feet and this time he knew nothing would hold her. If he were unwise enough to try, she would rake him with claws and sharp words. Twice he had stepped on the land mine of the subject of Johnny, only to have it explode in his face. Raine was trickier to handle than fulminate of mercury. He had only been used to women who were explosive in other ways! They, at least, were predictable, even boringly repetitive. Raine Fisher was not predictable.

Raine Fisher had just walked out of his office without another word, without a backward glance. Nick Hunter had always taken what he wanted. A woman's price had been cheap—passion and presents—and a golden handshake to smooth the path of parting. Raine Fisher wore no visible price tag and he remembered the old saying: If you have to ask the price, you can't afford the merchandise.

Raine's exit from Nick's office had been noted by other, less neutral eyes than Mrs. Bolt's. Selene had been on her way to Nick's office to discuss and protest the information she had just received from her agent. Her engagement at Nick's hotel had been terminated in favor of a more lucrative offer from a hotel in Las Vegas, "which might lead to bigger and better things," in the words of her agent. Her happy agent had assured her that the management of the hotel at which she was currently appearing had been most obliging about the early, and abrupt, cancellation of her current contract. They had assured him that obtaining a replacement, even on such short notice, for Selene's part of the show would prove no barrier to her quick acceptance of the new and financially attractive contract. They would not even invoke the penalty clause.

Selene's agent had been ecstatic. Selene was not. Her career goals had taken a dramatic new turn when Nick had taken her to bed, and, until the advent of Raine Fisher on the scene, things had been progressing nicely, Selene thought. Since the conniving Mrs. Fisher had appeared, nothing had gone right from Selene's viewpoint. Nick was angry. She hadn't seen him since he'd left her on the dance floor on that disastrous evening and he hadn't returned her messages. Had he been with that mealy-mouthed bitch? Well, even if he had, she wouldn't be able to give him what a woman like Selene Eason could, and the sooner Raine Fisher understood that, the better!

Raine was in no mood to be told anything by anybody. She was furious with herself, and not at all happy with the world in general. What was it about Nick Hunter that allowed him to slip through her defenses whenever he chose? She had adjusted to Johnny's loss, hadn't she, and yet Nick seemed to bring the scar which lay across the two halves of her existence, the before with and after without Johnny, to searing life again and again, making her long for what she could not have.

The two men could not have been more dissimilar, in looks and in personality. Johnny had been, before the destroyer had struck, inches over six feet, a muscular, sun-streaked blond, with twinkling blue eyes. There had been no cynicism, no dark corners in Johnny. He had been light and laughter and, in spite

124

of the maturity forced upon him by the fact of his illness, he had embodied youth, the golden, always sunny days of childhood.

Nick was shadow and storm cloud, thunder and elemental power. He possessed a primitive masculine sensuality, a lightly leashed savagery that a feminine counterpart deep within Raine both longed to and feared to release.

Raine was a highly sensual person. Taste, textures, colors, harmony—she registered sensations vividly. She had become a woman in Johnny's arms, but though their lovemaking had carried overtones of tenderness and passion, it had also embodied a frantic denial of fate. Raine could accept the reality of sexual desire, but in her own case it had always been roused only by and for a man she had loved deeply. She had thought that it would always be thus for her. Nick was her first experience with the unfixated yet rivetingly powerful raw sexual impulse that can ignite spontaneously, unleavened by tenderness, between a male human animal and his female counterpart.

She did not love Nick. She could not love Nick, because, to Raine, love implied commitment. She had no commitment to Nick, nor he to her. They were worlds and experiences apart.

Raine scowled down into the creamy depths of her coffee cup. Her thoughts had run around and around like mice on an exercise wheel all the while she was walking obliviously through the hotel lobby and into the coffee shop. With only a fraction of her conscious attention she had found a vacant booth and had placed an order with a waitress whose face she would have been unable to recognize if called upon to do so at a later hour. Now she sat, looking for answers, not sure what the questions were, face-to-face with a person she didn't even recognize as herself.

Unfortunately she was soon also face-to-face with a person whom she did recognize and wished that she didn't. Without a "Do you mind?" or a "Might I join you?" Selene Eason slid onto the seat opposite Raine and she didn't look as though getting a hot cup of coffee was the only thing on her mind.

Raine wasn't in a politely hypocritical mood. She didn't bother to give Selene a falsely welcoming smile nor did she ask what Selene had in mind. She was sure that she'd find out in due time and equally sure that finding out wasn't going to be a pleasant process for anyone concerned. Raine acknowledged privately that she was in the mood to bite the head off of a tenpenny nail. One bottle blond shouldn't present any problem!

Once again the two women presented a study in contrasts. Selene was dressed in a skin-tight violet jumpsuit with the zipper open almost down to her waist. Inch-long false eyelashes and three-inch heels topped and toed her and her nail polish matched her lip gloss, matched her eye shadow, matched her jumpsuit. She looked no different from, if somewhat more attractive than, a hundred other women of her type who frequented the purlieus of the high roller. Her silver-blond hair was casually arranged, so casually that it must have taken her an hour with a hair dryer and styling brush. As before, the contrast favored Raine.

Raine didn't immediately go on the offensive with

Selene as she had with Nick. She sipped her coffee and waited for the woman to carry the attack to her. She could parry any thrust Selene cared to make and she wasn't inclined to exert herself more than was minimally necessary.

Raine's provoking indifference to her presence seemed to infuriate Selene and her lips thinned into an ugly, sneering line. She dove wildly into the attack. "Why did you go to see Nick?"

Raine met the look of enmity that blazed from the narrowed eyes of the woman who sat so tensely across from her with cool composure. "That's none of your business, Selene. It didn't concern you in any way." Raine responded bluntly.

"Nick concerns me," Selene shot back. "He is my business and I want to know why you went to see him. He's my lover," she emphasized, just in case Raine hadn't gotten the message before, "and I have the right to know what happened between you two." She leaned back, satisfied that she had stated an irrefutable fact.

Raine regarded Selene with mingled pity and ill-concealed contempt. The woman was a fool. "Selene, whatever rights you have or feel you have with Nick are your business. You have no rights with me. My business with Nick was private and I'll tell you just once more that it had nothing to do with you or your relationship with Nicholas Hunter."

Selene's violet lips opened, but Raine cut across whatever words might have emerged with swift and brutal finality. "Take your rights to Nick, Selene, and ask him whatever questions you care to. I'll answer none of them."

Raine began to rise majestically. Her coffee was cold and her temper was hot. It was time she left before she let her heated temper goad her into pouring her cooled coffee over the head of the furious woman who was quivering with thwarted fury.

Selene was no quitter. Her hand flashed across the intervening space and clamped around Raine's wrist. Her fury gave her added strength and the bones and skin were painfully squeezed. Raine could feel the sharp points of Selene's nails gouging into the tender skin over the pulse in her wrist. Selene's claws were unsheathed and digging for heart's blood.

"What's the matter, Raine?" Selene hissed, a small scatter of moisture spraying from her lips like venom showering from the fangs of a spitting cobra. "Are your priggish morals offended or—" her purr was the snarl of a striking cat "—is it jealousy?"

Raine's eyes narrowed with unconcealed distaste and her nostrils flared and then contracted in controlled rage. She made a twisting, flickering motion with her imprisoned wrist and broke Selene's punishing grip.

Her voice was chillingly quiet but the rasping snarl of the female who was willing to repay claw for claw curled beneath her even tone. "I neither approve nor disapprove of your morals and sleeping arrangements, Selene. The only morals I am responsible for, thank God, are my own. I have less than no interest in yours or anyone else's—" the emphasis was telling "—and I sit as no judge or jury. The only time I interest myself in another person's code of honor, or lack of it, is when it impinges upon my own. You need have no fear of yours affecting me in any way," she finished dryly. "Do what you will with whom you will." It was a permission that drove Selene into a final frenzy.

"You lie!" Selene spat, her face flushing a mottled red. "You want Nick. I know it. Well, Mrs. Fisher, he is *mine!*" She was ragingly possessive. "He comes to *my* bed and leaves it sated. I give him all he needs in a woman and you can give him *nothing!*" Her eyes glittered feverishly and minuscule flecks of moisture bubbled at the corners of her lips. For a shivering instant even her hair seemed to writhe into Medusa-like tendrils.

Raine's repugnance at the ugly scene was complete. This time, unhindered by Selene's clutching grip, she rose and stood by the table, looking down. Her previous pity was totally replaced by disdain.

With convincing clarity Raine pronounced, "Nick can crawl from your bed on legs too weak to support him for all I care, Selene. I have no interest in competing with you for his attention. I give you this final warning. Do not continue to involve me in your petty jealousies and fears of being unable to hold your man. If Nick wants you, he'll take you, until he tires of you. It is nothing to me, or to do with me. I have another purpose here and when it is done, I will go my own way most gladly, but until that time, stay out of my way!" It was no threat. It was a promise. Raine would make Selene very sorry if Selene ever tried to subject her to another scene like the one she had just had to endure.

Raine spun on her heel and strode from the room, a grim set to her shoulders and a fighting tilt to her chin. If Nick Hunter was unlucky enough to cross her path any time soon, she'd mow him down just as the knife-wheeled chariots of ancient times and climes had decimated the hapless foot-soldiers of the opposing armies. Raine had just drawn blood from Selene and if some of Nick Hunter's got splashed around as well . . . well, too damn bad! Her teeth were so tightly clenched that her jaw hinges ached. She had a powerful urge to bite someone!

CHAPTER VI

Raine's incendiary explosion of blistering rage lasted much longer than was usual for her. Normally her temper was slow to ignite and short to burn on matters concerning her personal feelings, but there was nothing remotely normal about the situation she now found herself in. She had never been subjected to such a degrading scene, in public or in private in her whole life and her naturally fastidious sensibilities revolted. And though Nicholas Hunter had not been a direct participant, the whole ugly scene had been *his* fault. How *dare* he involve her, even indirectly, in his shoddy little intrigues!

Raine mentally muttered baleful maledictions as she stalked to the reception desk, penned a short note to Mary, and waited, with finger-drumming impatience, to be told that her car had been brought around to the front. She didn't plan to drive far, not in her current state of mind! She'd be a mobile menace to herself and to the other drivers on the road and Raine had more sense than to endanger lives, her own or others, out of sheer temper.

No, she wouldn't go far, but she just had to get away from people. A walk in the woods, a wade in the water. She'd find some private place where she could grind her teeth and unleash some of the choicer samples of invective she'd acquired during her varied travels. One especially appropriate and complicated malison had occurred to her, but it required speaking aloud to achieve the properly satisfying effect. The chances of someone around her understanding French, American unilingualism being what it was, were admittedly remote, but you never knew. It would be a shame to shock the socks off of some little old lady whose only crime was the innocent desire to break the arm of a one-armed bandit.

By now Raine was driving with courteous determination toward a place she had been told was both private and peaceful. She had intended, still intended, to bring Mary there to watch the sunrise, and perhaps a sunset, as part of her program to help the stricken woman come to terms with this crisis in her life, but for now it would serve to bring back some much needed tranquility to a sorely tried Raine.

Without too much trouble she found the spot. It was both private and scenic and would, later, do admirably for the proposed outings with Mary. It also served Raine's immediate needs. She scrambled up onto a large, upthrust rock, careless of the damage it might do to her immaculate appearance, and looked out over the lake, unconscious of the small lappings of water at her feet. Later they would soothe. Now only a few choice words would abate her choler.

She gave fluent tongue to the few choice words. The verbal expression of her inner perturbation was enormously gratifying. She denigrated Nick's morals

132

and manners with painstaking exactitude, covering past, present, and future iniquities. When she had finished, she felt relaxed and emptied, relieved, for the moment, of the strain and tension that had been building within her ever since Nick Hunter had looked at her, and dismissed her as negligible, at the Reno airport.

Raine had wasted no imprecations on Selene. Selene was nothing, a bagatelle, not worth a syllable or a phrase. Whether she knew it or not, Selene's moon had set, never to rise again on Nick's horizon. Her assault on Raine had been the reflexive death throe of her relationship with Nick. Dead as a dodo. Raine knew it, and if Selene didn't, she soon would the first time she confronted Nick, especially if Selene took him to task about his interest in the new woman, Raine Talbot Fisher.

It was several days before Raine and Nick were again in the same room at the same time. Chance or his intention, it achieved the same purpose. They didn't set eyes on each other.

Perhaps Nick had meant to allow a breathing space between the old and the new, or perhaps he was just lying low. Raine knew that he must have heard of her confrontation with Selene. It had been far too public for him not to have been informed, if Selene herself hadn't taken that chore in hand, to her undoubted discomfiture.

Selene had been replaced in the lounge. Another singer, male this time, crooned and breathed heavily into the microphone. The green suite was vacant, but Mary had far too much tact to even hint that Raine might enjoy the increased living space and more luxurious surroundings that the suite offered.

In spite of her increasing fragility, which was apparent to Raine because she was expecting and attuned to it, Mary radiated a perpetual, poorly hidden air of amusement and excitement. She was obviously deriving considerable satisfaction from her interpretation of recent events. Even if nothing else happened, Selene had been eliminated as a threat to Nick's long-term felicity. In Mary's judgment, better the devil you don't know, if the one you do know is named Selene Eason.

Raine gently guided Mary through such activities as the older woman found strength and heart for, including those that Raine had devised, based on her previous experience with Johnny. They talked, and not just on the philosophical subjects which might have been expected to absorb Mary's interest. Raine was perfectly willing to discuss philosophy, her own personal beliefs as well as the more abstract aspects of the various religions, major and minor.

Raine had traveled widely and everywhere she had gone, she had observed, and to a certain extent participated in, the daily lives of the people around her. For many of these peoples, religion, their own individual brand of it, had formed an integral part of their everyday existence. Raine had always respected and learned, even though she could not adopt the ideas for her own.

She could talk about them, but she could not inject them into Mary as some sort of vaccination against doubts. Mary would have to develop her own antibodies against the personal antigens of her fear of what is unknown and inherently unprovable.

As Mary gradually achieved a growing measure of acceptance and tranquility, Raine paradoxically found herself wrestling with an increasingly uncomfortable tendency to think about Nick. She hadn't seen him since that day of embarrassing infamy, but he was still at the hotel. He hadn't gone on one of his usual short, but routine, business trips, which, according to Mary, was most unusual. "Interesting," was the way Mary phrased it. "Suspicious" was Raine's sour, silent amendment.

He visited Mary each morning in her suite and saw her at irregular intervals during the rest of the day, but somehow, where Raine was, Nick wasn't. Mary mentioned casually, but with obvious pleasure, that this was the most attention she had ever received from Nick, and, even more auspiciously, that they seemed to be achieving a rapprochement hitherto unattainable in their previous relationship.

Mary didn't see fit to volunteer any information concerning Nick's continuing interest, or lack of it, in his mother's friend. Raine wouldn't ask. But it didn't stop her from wondering.

It was not a question of "if" but only one of "when." Nick Hunter hadn't finished with her . . . nor she with him, possibly. And that was the crux, the real core of her problem. She was coming to accept the fact that she was not yet finished with him. Somehow, against her will and in defiance of her prior certainties about the type of person she was, he had roused primitive urges that had been dead or sublimated for years. She responded to him on a level she had never plumbed before, nor had thought to. It was not love. It could not be love. Was it only lust? She winced away from the bitter ugliness of the word, but then, with remorseless honesty, she examined the concept.

She desired him. That was a fact. She would no longer clap her hands over her inner eye so that she might not be forced to look at truth. She had looked at truth before. It hurt sometimes, but willful ignorance changed nothing. So Raine Talbot Fisher desires Nicholas Anthony Hunter. Carve it in the bark of a tree, but encircle it with no heart pierced by a cupid's arrow.

Johnny had been a furry golden bear. Nick would be a sleek and silken puma, she imagined, only lightly black-dusted with body hair, a genetic heritage from his ancestors. Mary had confirmed the flow of Indian blood, diluted, but obviously still running through his veins. Raine's eyes took on a slumberous blue glow, an outward reflection of the inward sensual tenor of her thoughts.

With a sharp hiss of displeasure Raine yanked the plunging steed of her imagination to a halt. Imagination was not reality. Desire was not consummation. She had admitted to herself that she desired Nick. But that didn't mean she was going to sleep with him!

As thoroughly as he had disappeared, Nick suddenly became highly visible. He was everywhere. Their first meeting came at breakfast, with Mary as an interested observer. It was a non-event.

Raine and Mary had formed the habit of breakfasting in Mary's suite, both because of the seclusion

—neither was particularly gregarious by choice at the beginning of the day—and because of the informality of dress it allowed Mary, who could lounge comfortably in a caftan while she gathered her resources to meet another day. When Raine walked into the suite, responding to Mary's "Come on in, Raine," she noticed nothing amiss until she saw that the table was laid for three places.

"Would you pour the orange juice, Raine, dear?" Mary called from her bedroom. "I'll be with you in just a minute and—" A sharp double rap interrupted her. "That'll be Nick. Let him in, please," Mary continued lightly.

Raine sucked in a deep breath, let it out, and let Nick in.

He didn't seem surprised to see her, or at all disconcerted, but then Raine hadn't expected him to be. Nick greeted her casually but with just the right degree of appreciative warmth.

He didn't lift an eyebrow, but Raine knew that those dark eyes had thoroughly assessed the crisp white duck bellbottoms and the navy blue overblouse with its narrow white piping as well as the convex swell of breast and hip that they clothed. His voice didn't compliment her on her appearance, but his eyes did. Raine maintained a bland demeanor, but her placidity was only skin deep, and she suspected that he knew it.

From that beginning he was omnipresent—there at lunch, dinner, and breakfast again. He never put a foot or a word wrong. He never forced the pace and seemed content to allow her awareness of him as a man and as a person to ripen slowly. She got the message: *Take your time. We're in no hurry.* She also got another message, one which he probably didn't intend for her to pick up: *I can afford to keep to the slow pace because the outcome is never in doubt.* The confidence of *that* message made her bristle.

Raine didn't know whether to be relieved, regretful, or resentful. She could have resisted his insidious physical appeal to her senses much more easily had he tried to pressure her into a physical relationship she was not ready for.

Nick's campaign was far more subtle. He touched her lightly and frequently—a brush across the shoulder as he seated her at the table, a light warm touch of his fingers on her bare arm when he helped her to rise from the table after each meal Somehow he was *always* there before she could get up by herself. Little touches, each one casual, almost incidental, none a fraction of a second too long, and yet the cumulative effect was impressive.

Another aspect of his strategy was equally crafty, and just as hard to resist. He saw to it that she got to know the Nick Hunter behind the public face. She was introduced to the hard-headed businessman, to the man who had a dry and penetrating wit, and to the shrewd observer of the human scene. She also met the cynic, but, surprisingly, there was a touch of humanitarian as well, on occasion, although she had had to dig harder to uncover that particular persona.

He was well read and their taste in literature exhibited some unexpected congruencies. Their tastes in music also overlapped in many areas, although he loathed Von Suppé and Offenbach—he called them cliché music—and Raine detested whiny female country singers, or whiny male ones for that matter. He called her a musical snob, but he had grinned wickedly when he said it and she suspected that his devotion to country-western wasn't as all embracing as he had avowed.

He was a man of many facets (Had she met them all?), many of which were seductively attractive and some of which were just downright seductive. She didn't forget what she already knew of him, of his darker side, because that was a part of the man as well, but now there was light to balance against the dark. The oscillation of her opinion, now pro, now con, complicated by her unwilling attraction to him, kept her on edge. Raine could not be neutral. Nick would not allow it.

If Nick's plan to introduce himself to Raine was progressing without any major snags, the same could not be said of his project to learn more about this woman who intrigued and interested him. There were so many subjects he dared not approach except with the most devious of indirections, lest he find himself in the midst of another explosion, triggered by a clumsy misstep.

Mary, an obvious and logical source of information, had refused to perform her maternal duty. In so many words she had told Nick that what Raine wanted him to know about herself, she'd tell him. He had protested that some of it might come better from Mary because he'd already upset Raine once—a rather gross understatement on several counts—when he had asked about her husband.

"Ah, yes, Johnny," Mary had murmured musingly, her voice conveying many shades of emotion, none of them decipherable to Nick. She had glanced sharply over at her son and had been astonished to glimpse what could only be an unprecedented expression of chagrin and naked curiosity before he swiftly achieved impassivity again.

"I think," Mary had concluded gently, "that only Raine can tell you about Johnny."

"But Johnny is dead, isn't he?" Nick had pressed. He sought confirmation beyond a shadow of a doubt. Raine had said so, but there had been a strange and newly raw intensity to her words, as though she had just touched on a fresh grief.

"Yes, Johnny is dead. He's been dead for over five years." Mary had closed the subject firmly and Nick had not raised it again. He had had more than enough to think about for the present.

Raine sensed his dilemma, and did nothing to ease it. The subject of Johnny was not one she would discuss with Nick, certainly not now, perhaps not ever. She could appreciate the delicate precision with which he probed for information, always cautious lest he trigger a hidden explosive charge which would blow all of his plans to smithereens. She could, and did, relish circumventing him. Mary had been correct. Raine would tell Nick what she wanted him to know . . . and that was nothing.

He was free to deduce whatever he could from the Raine he knew as his mother's friend. He could draw his conclusions from her physical appearance and from what he already knew about her, but her past and her future were closed to him. He had the present. It should be enough for his purposes, Raine told herself grimly. She didn't imagine that he had required a life history from every woman he had made his mistress, and he wouldn't get one from her, whether or not she eventually decided to accept him as her lover.

Alas for Raine's determination to exclude Talbot from her sojourn at the hotel. She could no more cease recording the faces of the people around her than she could cease breathing. In point of fact, she could probably have dispensed with the latter less painfully than she could the former. The latter was necessary to the body. Painting was necessary to Raine's soul. It gave her purpose in life.

Unbeknownst to Mary, Raine was compiling a series of sketches of the older woman, recording the stages as she strove to achieve tranquility. They would culminate with an oil, which Raine had already begun. It would be her parting present to Mary, an accolade to her courage and, when the time came, a memento, a memorial of his mother for Nick, one which would express the finest aspects of her character, for it would be that way that he should remember her.

Mary, however, was not Raine's only subject. From the moment she had ducked into the casino to escape from Nick on that first evening, Raine had nurtured the seed of an idea for a collection of portraits, some almost caricatures, stark and spare in dramatic ink, and others in oils, richer in depth and dimension. The series as a whole would be titled: THE GAMBLERS.

Even during her first brief visit to the casino on that night, Raine had been struck by a similarity of the faces, not in bone structure or coloring, but in expression. She had confirmed her initial impression with subsequent visits and had concluded that it was due to an intangible common denominator, a complex tangle of emotions. Dice, cards, the roulette wheel, the triplet winners in the windows of the slot machines—any or all could evoke that intricate knot of asexual passion. Not all faces mirror-imaged that avid yearning, but of those who did, their name was legion.

In her spare time, in the afternoons while Mary rested, and in the evenings, after Mary had gone to bed, Raine had prowled, looking for faces. She had found them in the afternoon, mesmerized before the spinning shapes that flickered past the windows of the slot machines. At night, early or late, the faces could be found circling green felt tables, tables marked by lines and numbers, and tables on which wheels spun while small, frenzied balls jerked and danced to a staccato rhythm that clicked out a melody by which dreams were lost and won. Like wolves around a campfire, their eyes glowed in the smoky light, watching with feral intensity as the counters changed hands.

When she had found a face or a scene, she chose an inconspicuous vantage point and with a deft economy of line, began to record the essence of the personality. She was recording one such face with great intensity when Nick found her.

Mary was resting, as she had to rest more frequently these days. Raine had taken her into Reno that morning for an appointment with her doctor, who could tell her nothing new but who had been secretly amazed by the change in his patient, not in body, but in spirit. When they returned to the hotel after stopping on the way for a light lunch, Mary had gone immediately to her suite.

Raine had gone to her room, picked up a compact sketching pad and a supply of pencils and, after strolling casually through the ranked rows of slot machines, had established herself at a vantage point that offered partial concealment, not that her oblivious model would have noticed a tap-dancing blue elephant.

She had been sketching for some time, and the model had gone through an impressive amount of coins, including all the coins he had won from a small jackpot, when she finally laid aside her pencil and stretched her cramped fingers. She flexed her neck and upper spine and shook her arms and fingers to relax the tight muscles, half-bending at the waist as she did so.

When she straightened up, Nick was there.

A totally uncontrollable reflex sent guilty color spreading beneath her skin before she was able to regain her normal composure. She hoped that he'd think that it was due to her previous half-stooped position or even to a sudden flustered awareness of him in a physical sense, because he was very close, but she doubted it.

When she lifted her eyes to scan his face, she discovered that he wasn't looking at her at all. His eyes were fixed on the most recent sketch as it lay atop the half-fanned sheaf of previous sketches. Without a word he stretched forth a hand and gently spread the sheaf to more fully expose the remaining, individual studies and the incriminating color notes, which were revealingly professional. The face she had been capturing was one she had decided to render in oils because the patriarchal majesty of the bone structure was at such variance with the avid avarice that had contorted the expression.

When his attention returned to her, she warily tried to assess his reaction. Perhaps she could still regain control of the situation. There was no reason for him to know about or to connect her in any way with Talbot, and many people painted as a hobby.

"Security has been observing a woman who has been acting suspiciously—" his lips twitched but his eyes were unreadable "—for several days. I decided to have a look myself before we did something, if anything, about it." Nick's voice was cream-smooth.

Raine didn't think that he expected a comment from her. She could have kicked herself. Of course someone would have noticed her! She just hadn't thought about it! Or that Nick himself would have decided to investigate. Where there is money, where people spend, win, and lose small and large fortunes, there is security, and security personnel are born suspicious. Any deviation from normal activity is bound to be noticed and acted upon.

Carefully Nick stepped around her and just as carefully he gathered the separate sheets into a neat pile. He handed the pencils to the still mute Raine, but he kept possession of the drawings himself. *Is he holding them hostage?* Raine wondered with a tinge of gallows humor.

"Shall we go?" It was phrased as a question, but it allowed only one answer.

They didn't go to his office as she had expected they would. Instead Nick guided her through the lobby, his hand warmly cupped beneath her elbow, and into the corridor where the family quarters were located, past the door of the green suite, past Mary's suite, where he brought her to a halt before the discreet double doors that opened into his own domain. She wondered briefly why he hadn't chosen to occupy the hotel penthouse, but she didn't really care. She was just making idle mental conversation with herself, amassing her energies for the coming conversation, which wouldn't be idle.

With an artist's appreciation for color, but very little immediate interest in her surroundings, except for the location of the nearest exit, Raine surveyed the living room, all the while keeping one wary eye on Nick. Dark green silver-gray polished wood, and a deep-piled carpet that seemed to creep up around her ankles were the fragmentary impressions that impinged on her preoccupied brain just before Nick spoke and caused her to center the whole of her attention strictly on him.

"I'm through making false assumptions and jumping to hasty conclusions about you, Raine." Nick spoke with controlled vehemence. He looked down at the stack of drawings he still held in careful hands. He laid them down on an end table with a deliberate gesture and raked her with an exasperated gaze as she stood, poised but watchful, in the middle of his living room.

She didn't make any immediate comment and he continued, his tone matching his gaze. "I'm going to

145

ask . . . politely, if possible. Who *are* you, Raine Fisher?"

Raine tried the sweetly reasonable route. "I'm exactly who I said I was, Nick. My name is Raine Fisher and I'm a friend of your mother's. I assure you that I'm not traveling under an assumed name."

He snorted disgustedly. "I didn't think you were, but are you traveling under an assumed occupation?" Raine looked at him blankly. He must have slipped a cog somewhere. Nick explained precisely, each word pronounced clearly and distinctly, bitten off sharply by his strong, even teeth, "I mean, my dear Raine, that you deliberately fostered the impression that you had just spent a good deal of time in Mexico doing nothing more constructive than sifting sand through your toes! What occupation did you list on your passport application? Beachcomber? Or artist?"

"I do paint," Raine admitted reluctantly. Slowly but surely he was dragging the information forth, but she was determined to contest hotly each grudgingly released bit of data.

Nick closed his eyes for an instant, irritation and amusement warring for dominance on his dark face. "It's a shame that thumbscrews have gone out of fashion," he growled. "Well, judging from these sketches I can definitely not accuse you of hyperbole or overexaggeration. 'I do paint,' " he quoted her admission ironically. "I would say that you certainly do! Where do you *exhibit* ?" If that's the way she wanted it, that's the way they'd do it, one question, one answer, at a time. He could be patient and no one had ever accused him of lacking tenacity.

While Raine was trying to decide how best to evade answering that question, Nick sighed and commanded, "Have a seat, Raine. I'll get you a glass of wine. I'm sure your throat's dry from all the talking you've been doing."

The sarcasm was a little heavy footed, but considering the provocation she'd given, he felt he was holding to his temper reasonably well. He found it difficult to be urbane when what he really wanted to do was to wring the answers out of her as one might squeeze water out of a sopping wet sponge. He wanted her to gush, to deluge him with information and she seemed equally determined to dribble the facts forth one torturous drop at a time.

Raine chose a chair. No couches for her! Nick brought her a stemmed crystal goblet of dry white wine and observed the seat she had chosen with a sapient eye. He forbore from commenting, but the slight shake of his head was ruefully eloquent. She wouldn't allow him any advantage.

Had his thought been voiced aloud, Raine would have agreed wholeheartedly. She certainly *wouldn't* allow him such an advantage! Her reaction to his proximity was difficult enough to control when he was half a room away. She'd be a fool to sit right next to him on the couch! There was always the chance that he might be able to interpret correctly the motives behind her resolute avoidance of any physical contact with him. She'd removed her elbow from his grasp as soon as the opportunity had offered a natural excuse, but he might equally likely attribute it to a disinclination to be touched by any man, she hoped.

Raine understood her adversary. If Nick ever became certain that she desired him, he'd be the one who said when and his when would be right then! Raine couldn't, wouldn't, allow that. When, *if* . . . she wanted to be the one who made the decision. For her own sake, she must be the one who made that decision.

Nick fixed himself a light drink and took a seat on the couch. He didn't relax back against it, though, but instead he leaned forward, resting his elbows on his knees and regarding Raine steadily over the rim of his glass. He scanned her face for a long, silent minute and Raine felt an increase in the pace of the breath rushing in and out of her lungs. He was like a magnet, pulling every cell in her body toward a corresponding cell in his own.

It frightened her, this cellular draw of elemental need. It was beyond her previous experience and in her saner moments, which seemed to come less and less frequently, she feared its power. She was too proud to be a slave.

Nick sensed Raine's increasing antagonism, although he couldn't immediately divine its cause. Although she didn't realize it, Raine's face was expressive, to Nick at least. He'd made a determined effort to interpret every fleeting expression. He had to. She certainly wouldn't give him any clues to her feelings voluntarily.

It was time to increase the pressure. She was rebuilding her bulwarks, higher, broader, and stronger. He wanted to break through, to drive into the innermost citadel of this defensive yet strangely defenseless woman, not to master her, but to compel her to match him, in passion, in necessity. God knows he needed, wanted, her. She must, she *had to* want him!

"Raine," he stated with conviction, "you aren't an amateur painter. I've seen that style before. I can't remember where right now, but believe me, I will remember. If necessary I'll keep one of your sketches and take it to a friend of mine who's somewhat of an expert." Nick's smile was wolfish. "He owns the Delgarde Galleries in Phoenix, Tucson, and Albuquerque. If he doesn't recognize your work immediately, he can put me in touch with someone who will."

Raine glared at him. He laughed. "You know you can't stop me if I want to keep one of those sketches, and if you don't tell me what I want to know before you leave this room, my secretive and exasperating lovely lady, believe me, I will take the sketch and it'll be in the mail to Rafael Delgarde tonight."

Raine glanced at the pile of sketches speculatively. The temptation to scoop them up and run for it was intense but it was also impractical, undignified, and futile. He'd catch her and, worse, enjoy doing it.

She played her last card. "Why must you know, Nick? Am I not entitled to my privacy?"

He trumped it without mercy. "No. Why do you feel that you must defend your privacy so vigorously?"

She didn't want him going further down that avenue of speculation. "You're not being fair," she complained hastily, to distract him from the subject.

The lift of his dark eyebrow was mocking and it made her long to hit him. "Who said I had to be fair, Raine? My rules don't require it and we're playing by my rules. The first and only rule in this game is that I win. We're in Nevada, my lovely, where gambling is legal and the thing to remember is that the house *always* wins in the long run." His smile was teasingly complacent. "I own the house."

"I told you that I don't gamble, Nick," Raine said sharply, hoping to stave off the inevitable just a little longer.

"All of life is a gamble, darling." His voice dropped to a husky half-whisper and his eyes caressed her face with an almost physical intensity. "You are very much alive."

Raine capitulated abruptly. Much more of this verbal seduction and she'd be a goner. It was Mary's fault. Why couldn't her son have been short, paunchy, and unattractive instead of being, as the saying went . . . one to suicide oneself for! The demise Nick offered her was the little death, infinitely pleasurable and *almost* irresistible. A vagrant, ribald phrase floated into her consciousness. *What a way to go!*

It wasn't really funny. She'd just lost another round. Raine had no trouble subduing her momentary impulse to smile at her mental meanderings. The look she gave Nick was not humorous in the least. "My name is Raine Talbot Fisher," she said icily, the words, if not the tone of voice, echoing what she had said to Mary on the day she had saved her life and had generously offered succor to her troubled spirit. Now Raine was the one in need of succor. Who would rescue her? Did she need it? Did she want it?

"Talbot?"

"Talbot." Raine reached over and picked up one

150

of the preliminary sketches. She slashed the distinctive signature across the lower right-hand corner, got up, walked close enough to the couch to hand it to Nick, and then retreated to her chair.

He looked down at the paper in his hand and back up to meet Raine's unfriendly expression. "I thought Talbot was a man."

"Most people do."

"I thought Talbot . . . you—" he stumbled verbally "—must be older."

"I am. Sometimes I'm a thousand years old," Raine said quietly, looking down into some deep and private hell. "I've seen things that have made me a sister to Methuselah. I was in Bangladesh. I have walked the streets of New Delhi and of the Levant."

"You titled that series SUFFER THE CHILDREN, didn't you?" His perception should have surprised her, but it didn't. "And Unicef used it for one of their fund-raising efforts. Where are the originals?" He was curious, but he also wanted to lead her away from the edge of the pit she stared into as she remembered the living models.

"A private collector bought the series as a whole and donated it to the National Gallery in Washington, D.C." She answered him absently. The money from the sale, plus considerably more from the coffers of the Fishers and the Talbots, had gone to buy food for the children, and their brothers and sisters. Raine had not walked away from the children. She had left a piece of her spirit behind and had carried away the memories.

Raine seemed to have forgotten him and her surroundings. She looked toward a Dupré spiral etching

151

hung on the wall to the left of Nick's head but he doubted that she saw it. "Raine?" and then more sharply, "Raine!" He would not allow her to escape into her past. This was here. This was now, and she was Raine Fisher, not Talbot. Talbot was the artist. It was Raine Fisher whom he wanted in his arms.

Raine's reflexes were slowed. By the time she had registered the sharp command, the warning of imminent action in Nick's crisp repetition of her name, it was too late.

The chair was no asylum. With authority, with ease, Nick scooped her up from her haven and carried her back over to the couch, where he had intended to have her from the first.

Raine came out of her abstraction immediately. "Put me down!" she ordered.

"Certainly." He complied with a dangerous grin and dropped her gently onto the couch. By the time she had bounced down, he had followed her and had consolidated his superior tactical position.

His hands framed her face, gently, possessively. "I'm going to kiss you, Raine." He told her what she already knew. "I took a kiss before, which, I think, was not mine to take." Now his voice was thoughtful and a little sad.

Raine's eyes widened in shock and a cold chill ran down her spine. How could he know? It was almost as though he had crawled inside her mind and read the thoughts etched in the protoplasm of her brain.

"Give me a kiss of my own, Raine," Nick commanded her softly. "Give me what is *mine*."

He was right. There was a kiss which was his

alone, and had been his for days now. Her arms slid up around his neck, noting in passing the depth of the muscle that covered the broad, hard bones of his shoulders, but her attention was focused on his mouth. Her lips shaped, parted to receive him, while her eyelids drifted shut to seal her within a dark, warm world of taste and touch and the exciting, lightly musky smell of an aroused male.

There was no coy, maidenly insincerity in the kiss Raine gave to Nick. With a woman's generosity she shared the intimacy that he both took and gave back. The special taste which was Nick lingered on her tongue, and with the scent of his skin, registered in her brain to form a composite, highly personal, sensory memory of Nick Hunter. There were other ways to augment such a memory-picture but she was not ready for that.

Nick's tongue stroked gently and then withdrew from that deeper intimacy to trace the softly full outline of her lips. He kissed her closed lids and then whispered, "Raine, darling, open your eyes. Look at me."

Her slumberous lids lifted slowly, and the dark expanded wells of her pupils reflected the miniaturized image of the intensely masculine face that hovered above her. He filled her eyes. There was only Nick.

"Was that *my* kiss, Raine? Only mine?" His voice was low, but she could not mistake the urgency.

"Your kiss, Nick," she assured him throatily. "Only yours."

His sigh of satisfaction brushed over her skin. "I'm

glad," he said simply. "I'll take nothing more for now." Once before he had grabbed at something that was not his, only to have it turn to bitter ash in his hands. He would not make the same mistake with Raine again.

CHAPTER VII

Raine was confused. Why had Nick let her go after only one kiss? It was certainly not for any lack of desire on his part, or hers. She was too experienced not to recognize the signs of a man's full arousal. He had wanted her, and with a certain amount of skillful persuasion on his part, could have finished what he had so expertly begun.

Instead, he had helped her to sit up, had retrieved her scarcely touched glass of wine, and had sat beside her on the couch, close but not too close. While she sipped he finished his own drink in several large swallows. He set his glass aside and half turned to face her.

"Raine, I'd like to talk to you." There was an almost hesitant quality to his words, as though he felt he must carefully select the phrases he used. Raine stiffened suspiciously. Now what?

Nick recognized her defensive reaction. She was so terribly wary of him and his intentions. And she had cause, he admitted to himself. What he wanted, he suspected that she would be unwilling to give.

"Has Mary said anything to you . . . ? That is, has

she mentioned . . . ?" He fumbled for words, not sure how to phrase his question.

Now he had Raine's full attention. Whatever she had thought, she had not thought that he would speak of his mother. "Has Mary said what?" she prompted.

"Is she feeling all right?" he questioned bluntly.

"What makes you think she isn't?" Raine parried his question with her own, trying to decide what to tell him. At one time she had resolved to tell Nick about his mother's illness if it would help Mary, but the situation was different now. Nick was more than she had thought him to be. Now she believed that he and Mary could be left to work out their complicated relationship between themselves, without her interference. And yet she could not lie to him. She could not say that all was well with Mary when it was not, nor would be.

"She's been losing weight." Nick listed one obvious portent. "She seems to tire so easily and, oh, I don't know . . ." He waved a hand expressively but helplessly. "She's changed. I noticed it when she came back from San Francisco. She seemed smaller, shrunken somehow, and subdued."

He raked the long fingers of one hand through his thick straight hair in the first gesture of uncertainty she'd ever seen him make. She suppressed the instinct to smooth the rumpled black strands.

"And that's the most noticeable thing," he continued, the puzzlement in his voice growing with each word as he expressed aloud the things he had noticed but had not really considered as parts of a whole, and very disturbing, picture. "She's subdued, or perhaps that's not quite the correct word. She seems to have acquired serenity. My mother has never had serenity." There was a dry and painful bitterness moving underneath his voice.

Raine felt her throat go tight with perceptive compassion. The little boy, betrayed by those who should have loved him best, afraid to love, afraid to trust, paying still for other people's mistakes—not that he hadn't made some of his own—she thought tartly, leavening her pity with realistic common sense. There comes a time in every life when others can no longer be called to account for the choices made, the paths trod. Nick had walked down his own path for a long time. She would keep her pity for the little boy who had stepped through a bedroom door and brought down his world on his head.

"Nick, I can't answer your question." It was "won't," but her controlled voice didn't reveal the important difference. "Have you asked Mary if there's anything wrong? She's the one you must talk to, not me."

There was gentle finality in her last sentence and Nick knew that he would get no more answers to his questions, at least on that subject. It would seem that his mother and Raine were going to be equally uncommunicative about each other's business. It was a feminine conspiracy that a mere male found impossible to combat.

When she had finally attained the privacy of her quiet room that evening, Raine knew that the time had come for her to make her decision. Her body had almost made it for her that afternoon, and only

Nick's incomprehensible restraint had kept the question from being strictly academic. She was grateful to him, but she wouldn't count on his forbearance on another occasion.

Mary would tell Nick soon, about everything, and their relationship would enter its final phase as mother and son, but also, if they both tried, they could meet the coming crisis as two adults who of late, but not too late, have come to like and respect each other.

Then Raine would be free to go. She had given Mary all she could, what wisdom she had learned from Johnny, what strength the simple act of caring would convey. Her conscience would release her now. She could go home until the restless spirit drove her out into the world again.

She would not be abandoning Mary. If the doctor were to be believed, Mary had months, a year or more, and the spirit was a potent fighter on the side of life. Raine would come to Tahoe on her way out into the world and each time she returned to see her family for as long as Mary needed her, was here to receive her.

So that left Nick.

What was she going to do about Nick? She had never considered that she might one day coolly decide to begin an affair. Well, perhaps coolly was not quite the phrase. Thoughts of Nick made her blood run anything but cool! That was the whole problem.

Her very nature rebelled against an affair. The commitment of her body to intimacy with a man was not a light thing for Raine. She had made that commitment only once. Could she make it again, knowing from the start that it was to be a temporary commitment, a meeting of the flesh, while the minds and spirits remained alienated?

Back and forth her mind and her body warred. There were ways to give herself ease, but they would not erase the longing for the length and warmth of a strong man's body covering her, weighing her down with bone and hard flesh, lifting her with strong and knowing hands to the sensate heights of release. And not just *any* man's hands, mouth, and body. Nick's hands, Nick's mouth, and Nick's lean, firm body. None other tempted her.

She washed her hair in the shower and then soaked for a long, languorous time in the warm scented tub of water in which she had dissolved several jewel-clear bath oil beads. She had hoped that the bath would relax her, but it merely sent a flush of sensuous warmth over her body as the water lapped and flowed over her sensitive, sensitized skin.

She dried her hair, smoothed lotion over her skin, and slipped into a sheer, pale blue cotton robe. When circumstances permitted, that is, when her sleeping accommodations were private and not shared with animals, children, and the families who were her hosts in their one-room homes, she slept nude. She enjoyed the pagan sensation of free air flowing over each square inch of her skin. Even in the coldest weather she preferred to burrow beneath layers of blankets, to warm her own small pseudocave with her body's heat rather than to encumber herself with smothering night garments.

The artificial chill of the air conditioning had raised goose pimples over her water-heated skin and the light weight of the full-sleeved robe would keep her comfortably warm until she was ready to sleep. Unfortunately, sleep was most certainly going to prove elusive unless she forced herself finally to come to grips with the perplexity that was her relationship with Nick.

She moved restlessly within the confines of her room, the long skirt swirling around her legs and ankles. She ran a hand over the slick texture of the wood-grained dresser, lifted and laid aside the book she had been reading, and moved to stand before the television, hesitating and then turning away. She couldn't find comfort there.

Nothing was going to distract her, she admitted finally, with a moue of wry resignation. She could not procrastinate any longer. She must at last face the decision that had been inevitable, the one she had refused to admit to herself consciously. She could not begin an affair with Nick, and an affair was all that was possible for either of them.

There. It was acknowledged. She felt a type of mournful relief akin to the sensation one feels when a thick and painful splinter is removed from beneath the skin. The pain from the wound still lingers, throbbing, but since the splinter is gone, the wound can at least begin to heal.

Desire for Nick still throbbed, and would until she was far from him in both distance and time. She knew from experience that time and distance are slow but effective analgesics and if a scar remained as a reminder of the experience, well, it would not be the only one she bore. Everything in life must be paid for one way or another.

Within a day or so Nick would confront Mary and ask his questions. Mary would answer them. Once that had happened, Raine's self-imposed duty would be done. Until then she had only to avoid the possibility of a tête-à-tête with Nick. Tomorrow she would call her parents and tell them that she was, at last, coming home.

Once the decision had been made, Raine thought she could sleep. She brushed her teeth, took off her robe, and laid it on the chair near her bed. She crawled into bed, shivering slightly as the cool, fresh sheet settled down in a soft billow over her bare skin. A quick pressure turned off the lamp and she stretched, shifting her hips slightly to find a comfortable position. In the darkness, silent except for the breathy hum of the air conditioner, she closed her eyes.

She must have dozed, or even slept, because the bright flood of light disoriented rather than alerted her. Her eyes flickered open briefly and then squinted shut against the sharp glare from the overhead fixture, trying to adjust to the sudden transition from dark to light, from sleep to full awareness. The second time she opened her eyes they stayed open. She rolled to her side and propped herself on her elbow, gazing around the room in bewilderment, looking for the cause of her abrupt awakening.

She hadn't far to look. Nick stood just inside her door, his hand still resting on the switch plate that controlled the overhead lights. She blinked several times, just to see if he'd disappear between blinks, but he didn't. He stood there, staring across the room at her.

He wore dark trousers—they were probably the ones from the suit he'd worn earlier when the three of them had dined in the restaurant—and the shirt was certainly the same except that he'd removed his tie and unbuttoned the first four buttons so that it gaped open halfway down his chest.

She'd been right, she noted dazedly. His skin was smooth and darkly bronzed. To touch him, to slide her fingertips across the layered muscles of his chest might feel like stroking over satin-finished wood, but a living wood which pulsed beneath her hand, vibrant and vital.

She could sense the tension in him. It reached out to her across the width of the room. Raine shook her head slightly, trying to bring order to her muddled, undisciplined thoughts. She wasn't fully awake and she was missing some vital factor. She stared more closely at his face and what she saw there sent her hand to her throat in an unconscious gesture of distress. He looked agonized.

She bolted upright, clutching the top sheet to herself automatically but not really conscious of anything except the naked anguish engraving deep furrows on Nick's forehead and cheeks. "Nick!" she gasped. "Is it Mary?"

"Yes, it's Mary." His voice was choked with emotion, hoarse and rasping, totally unlike his usual deep baritone.

Frantic concern galvanized Raine. Had Mary collapsed? Died? She was preparing to slip from the bed to go to her friend when Nick's next words halted her impulsive motion. "Why didn't *you* tell me? Damn

162

it, *you* knew! She's my mother. You should have told me!"

He swayed slightly and a shudder shook him momentarily. "Why didn't you tell me, Raine?" She heard the past echoes of the cry of a young boy, hurt and needing comfort, needing reassurance that he was important in the lives of those he loved.

Raine had to respond. Magnificently impervious to her state of undress, she threw back the sheet and rose from the bed. She walked over to the chair where her robe lay and slipped into it, tying the broad, flowing sash at the waist with steady fingers. She was concerned with far more important things than how much of her skin he could see.

She walked over to him. He hadn't moved, except for his eyes, which had followed her every motion. With gentle fingers she took the hand that seemed glued to the light switch, curling her smaller hand over his, and pulled it down, retaining her hold even when the clasped hands dropped heavily to his side.

With her free hand she switched off the overhead light, depending on the softer illumination of the bedside lamp to light their path into the room. Standing this close to him she could smell the sharp odor of alcohol, but she knew that he wasn't drunk, just in shock.

"Come sit down, Nick," she urged softly. "We'll talk about it."

She tugged lightly at the linked hands to emphasize her words, but he seemed unable to move. He had gotten to her room, but the impetus that had driven him could carry him no farther. "Come with me, Nick," she repeated.

This time he responded, although not in the way she had expected. He released her hand, but she was still not free. His arms swept around her, pulling her to him with desperate force. He buried his face in her neck and his arms wrapped around her, binding her against his body as though he could never let her go.

"Help me, Raine," he groaned, his words muffled against the side of her throat, and she was sure that she could feel the scalding drip of a bitter grief dampening her skin where his eyes rested against her.

Raine's arms slid around his back, pressing him closer, moving in a rhythmic, kneading motion that conveyed a wordless understanding. He had come, instinctively, blindly, to her for comfort. She had had Johnny and her families. Nick had no one. He could not go to Mary. He must give strength *to* Mary, not drain it *from* her. There was only Raine, and so he had sought her, needing her to help him through the first nightmarish hours as he struggled to accept his mother's mortality.

Raine could not turn him away. Her deepest instincts reached out to him, and she would ease his pain any way she could. She didn't protest when he swept her into his arms and carried her toward the waiting bed. Instead she wrapped her arms around his neck and laid her head against his shoulder in a silent signal of acquiescence.

Nick stopped by the edge of the bed and looked down at the woman who lay so pliantly in his arms. Her head rested confidingly against his shoulder and her arms entwined softly around his neck, pressing warmly against his skin. Her body was a golden shadow beneath the thin fabric of the robe that draped and contoured the curve of breast and thigh but did not conceal the womanly fullness.

His head dipped, nudging under her chin to tip her head back to expose the vulnerable curve of her throat. Obediently, Raine allowed her head to tilt back, offering the arch of her neck in a gesture of submission as ancient as time.

His lips traveled over her scented skin, relishing the delicate flavor of her flesh while he savored the completeness of her surrender to his urgent compulsion to possess her. Raine offered more than mere physical release for his body. In her arms he might find tranquility for his soul.

Like a sacrifice on an altar, Nick laid Raine on the bed and then straightened up again to gaze down at her outstretched figure with hungry satisfaction. The light robe had fallen back as he had placed her on the bed, baring the long line of her legs to a tantalizing height. As he loomed above her, he might have been a pagan priest, the high cheekbones and high-bridged nose labeling him a throwback to a more savage age. His dark eyes glittered, but he would plunge no steel-cold knife into her living body.

Silently, but with deft fingers, he untied the sash at her waist and spread the two halves of the robe apart, revealing the rich extent of the offering before him. Framed by the blue backdrop of her robe and the golden flow of her unbound hair, Raine waited quietly, her eyes watching him, welcoming him. The deep blue eyes were not yet languorous with desire, but her expression promised that, when the time came, she would burn with a flame as hot as his own.

Before he had removed more than his shirt, he

165

paused and stretched forth a hand to trace, with a gentle finger, around the rose-dusky circumference of a nipple that proudly crested a firm, ripe breast. He had touched her as though to confirm the reality of what his eyes feasted upon, but the responsive darkening of her eyes and the equally revealing firming of the inviting tip released his breath in a sigh which was almost a groan.

Raine watched him throw aside the rest of his clothes and stand before her, above her, beautiful as a man is beautiful, with the hard symmetry of muscle that complements and completes a woman. The tanned copper of his smooth skin clung tightly over the muscled breadth of his chest and outlined the sleek bulge of power in arm and thigh.

He did not lie down to cover her, claim her, at once. Instead he slid a broad palm beneath her back and lifted her slightly, pulling away the robe so that the contrast became one of gold against the white of the sheet. He tossed the blue drift of fabric carelessly aside and knelt beside the bed, prepared to worship on the altar of her body.

With tongue and hands and words he paid homage. Generously Raine accepted the adoration of her not-so-humble suppliant and generously she opened the treasures of her body to his questing hands and mouth.

She became a feast for his senses and when his mouth met hers in a deep and open kiss, there was the taste of honey, sweet on his lips. His hands stroked and teased, fondling and cupping the hand-filling curve of her breasts, brushing across the taut

166

tips of her nipples with his palms to arouse and tantalize them both.

No victim ever came more willingly to the impalement and when Nick drove into her body, Raine rose to meet and welcome his deep thrust. His hands slid beneath the curved arcs of her hips, lifting her so that he might join them more thoroughly. Raine arched into his driving demand, meeting it with her own instinctive rhythm that intensified and augmented the increasingly imperative, mutual need for fulfillment.

From some far-off place Raine registered the hoarse, gasping cry heralding Nick's release. His almost painful articulation of her name echoed her triumphant enunciation of the short syllable of *his* name, repeated with diminishing intensity as the inexorable paroxysm of mind-blanking ecstasy slowly released its grip on them both.

For a long, breathless time Nick's body lay heavily atop hers, slack in the total muscular relaxation of complete release. Then he lifted himself to one side, leaning on his elbow, relieving her of the full burden of his not inconsiderable weight. With a tender hand he smoothed the strands of her hair back from her damp forehead and whispered in a wondering voice, "You called my name." He dropped a kiss on her half-parted mouth and repeated, deep emotion roughening each word, "I heard you call *my* name."

She was torn with tenderness. Her hands reached up to frame the hard contours of his lean face. "I know who holds me, Nick. I know who gave me pleasure and who lies beside me now. There is no one in this bed but you and me." She traced over the dark wing of his eyebrow, trailing a light fingertip down to the corner of his mouth. She brought her hand over to her own lips, kissed the pad of her index finger and transferred the kiss to the center of his lips with a gentle pressure. "That kiss is yours also."

She smiled, daring to tease him gently. "You called my name as well. I remember!" She pulled his head down, initiating a long, sensual kiss, and when she let him go, both he and she were breathing deeply. "That is *my* kiss, is it not?" she questioned him with mock severity. "It bears no other's name, does it?"

His eyes registered the aptness of the hit, but his reply wasn't accompanied by the light smile she had expected. "All of my kisses bear your name, Raine." It sounded uncomfortably like a pledge.

Long after the light had been turned out, Raine lay awake, tucked into the possessive curve of Nick's body while he slept heavily beside her. She stared out into the darkness and her lips curved with an ironic twist. She had no one to blame but herself. And yet, in a strange way, she did not regret it.

It would make it easier, and yet harder, to go, and of course, she must go, now more than ever. The blending of their bodies had changed nothing. Nick had needed her, had come to her in an attempt to affirm life. She had taken his pain as her own and had given him the anodyne he craved, unable to withhold, to deny them both. No, she did not regret it, but she would not repeat it. Tonight was all they would have.

Even in the heat of the moment, when sweet words

and promises are cheap, their lovemaking had been silent. He had cried her name aloud but there had been no attestations of love, no promises, no vows. They had shared a coruscating passion. Together they had ridden the spiral into ecstasy . . . and that was all.

Nick had never whispered "I love you." He hadn't even declared "I want you," although his body had said it most effectively for him! Instead he had groaned, "Help me."

Now Raine begged wordlessly as she stared blindly out into the quiet darkness of her room while Nick dreamed peacefully beside her. *Let me go. Let me go home to those who love me.* She had calculated the cost required of her, the price she was paying for her impulsive action that had wrenched destiny awry on that San Francisco street. Raine had just discovered that the reckoning had rapidly escalated far past her ability to pay.

There was no barrier to her departure. At last Nick would be able to give Mary the emotional support she would need in the coming days. Mary would not need Raine.

Before he had fallen into a deep and tranquil sleep, Nick had recounted his conversation with his mother, the conversation which had been directly responsible for his presence in Raine's room . . . and her bed. Raine examined every aspect of the terse words Nick had used to describe the painful, but long overdue, revelations that Mary had poured forth.

With meticulous honesty Mary had revealed the circumstances that had been responsible for her marriage to Tony. She had delineated Tony's reaction to his unwilling participation in a shotgun wedding and had, for the first time, revealed to Nick his father's subsequent methods of reprisal against his hapless bride. Mary had lightly sketched the years of jealous anguish, the growing disillusion, and the inexorable death of love. She hadn't tried to excuse her own attempt at revenge on a husband who had flaunted his many infidelities, but at last she had been able to express to her son how deeply she had, and, still, regretted that he had been the one to pay the price for her ill-fated retaliation.

There had been little time for Nick to absorb this new interpretation of the events of his childhood that had so molded his adult character. Mary had seized the opportunity and, while the iron was hot, she had struck. It was because of the unexpectedness of the blow she had dealt him that he had fled into Raine's arms.

With no preliminary preparation Mary had announced that she was dying.

She had then gone on to expound on the events leading to her first encounter with Raine and her subsequent plea that Raine stay with her while she adjusted to her altered circumstances. Mary had evidently touched lightly on Raine's special qualifications for the task of helping the stricken woman get through the first difficult days, but Nick didn't dwell on that aspect of his mother's recapitulation. Raine shrewdly suspected that Nick was being careful not to raise the ghost of her husband between them. Raine's sad smile in the darkness was singularly mirthless. It was not a ghost who would send her traveling toward the sun at the first opportunity. It was Raine herself.

Even while he spoke, Raine had sensed that Nick was beginning to come to terms with his mother's illness. He had been jolted by Mary's blunt revelations, but Nick was resilient. He had the strength to cope with Mary, and, more importantly, Raine believed that he had the necessary compassion as well. She would not have credited it at first, but now she knew him better . . . much better. She could leave Mary in his hands. They would be gentle hands.

Raine dozed lightly for what remained of the night, always conscious of the warm length of Nick's body as it curved around her back. She had tried to edge away after he had settled into the depths of slumber, but he would not let her go. His body moved automatically to follow hers, almost as though he had triggered a subconscious alarm to ensure that she could not escape him.

Raine's internal time clock woke her at her usual hour. Nick still slept quietly beside her, but the tightly possessive clasp of his arm had slackened, so she was able to ease out of bed cautiously without rousing him. With a gesture an onlooker might have termed almost maternal, she tucked the sheet and blanket back around him. Appearances were deceptive. She didn't feel maternal, but she was afraid the loss of body heat would waken him before she was ready. She wanted to be showered and dressed before she faced him again. She would need all the psychological leverage she could get!

On stealthy feet she crossed the room. She selected

fresh underclothes, a crisp cotton shirt, and tailored slacks, and whisked into the bathroom just as Nick began to stir restively in the bed. Raine locked the door behind her with a decisive click.

She didn't dawdle, but she didn't rush either. She soaped and scrubbed her body thoroughly, but she couldn't really wash away the memories of the night before. Those would be with her for the rest of her life. The final effect was something less controlled than she had striven for. She'd forgotten to bring in a brush and she had no shoes, but it was infinitely better than bare skin! And he might even have gone back to his own suite by the time she came out.

He hadn't. He was lounging on the bed, his arms crossed behind his head, looking engagingly rakish and well rested. His smile was sensually intimate.

At least he was dressed. He'd donned his rumpled clothes from the night before and Raine was relieved to note that he'd even put on his shoes and socks. A man bent on early morning dalliance doesn't bother with his footgear. Even though he hadn't shaved and his clothes were creased—when he'd stripped them off the night before they had lain where they'd fallen —he still managed to exude an undiminished aura of attractive vitality.

"You locked the door," he chided her. "I was going to shower with you." His lambently glowing eyes silently told her what else he had planned to do with her, had she given him the chance.

In spite of herself, Raine blushed.

Nick laughed, his deep chuckle showed he was thoroughly amused. He had a feeling that it would be a rare occasion when he could discomfit the self-possessed Raine. She was such a contrast this morning, the clean formality of her crisp shirt and slacks so thoroughly belied by the vulnerability of her bare feet and tumbled hair. He rose smoothly to his feet.

"Nick, I—" Raine began hurriedly.

"No, you're right," he interrupted her. He scraped a rueful hand over his chin and then shoved a lock of hair back from his forehead. "I've got to shower and shave, and Mary'll expect both of us to share breakfast with her."

Raine tried once more. "Nick, I think . . ."

He stepped across the distance separating them and circled her waist with his arms, scraping his stubbled chin teasingly down the side of her throat while she struggled to finish her sentence.

"Nick!" she yelped, wriggling desperately to fend away the nibbling lips that were traveling so relentlessly down toward the open V of her shirt while his hands swept up from her waist to cup and gently compress the sides of her breasts, enticingly exaggerating the deep curves of the cleavage he nuzzled so hungrily.

"Mmmm," he mumbled into the voluptuous cleft he had created, and she felt the brief, burning lick of his tongue as he tasted her soap-fresh skin. "D'you think that Mary would notice if neither of us turned up for breakfast?" He enticed her with an exaggeratedly hopeful leer.

Raine gave up. He wasn't going to let her finish a sentence, but she knew, with equal certainty, that he had no immediate intentions of consummating his sensual teasing. Concern for Mary was uppermost in both of their minds and both of them would breakfast with Mary as usual.

"If you're going to shower and shave, and especially shave—" Raine scratched a light nail over the bristles along his jaw line "—before breakfast, you'd better go now." Keep it light, she advised herself silently. There'll be time for the heavy drama later.

Nick stopped nuzzling, but he still held her dangerously close. The danger was to her peace of mind. The heady scent of his skin, the lean warmth of his long body were both too evocative of the night before. She kept telling herself that this was the morning after, but her body didn't want to listen!

"It's unnatural when a woman is both logical and right," Nick complained from the region of her left ear. He sighed with exaggerated patience and kissed the tip of her nose before he reluctantly released her.

Raine couldn't resist the retort, "It's better than being logical and wrong," and then regretted it immediately when he corrected her with the outrageous response, "No, it's even better being in bed with you!"

Raine groaned. "You're hopeless!"

With a lightning shift in mood, Nick said gravely, "No. Once I might have been, but now I'm not. Not since I met you, Raine." His hand cupped her chin and tilted her face up so that she had to meet his eyes fairly. "You're a very special person, Raine Talbot Fisher. I'm glad you came into my life."

He dropped his hand, smiled warmly at her, and went out the door, whistling "I'm in the Mood for Love" with trills and flourishes, leaving a shaken

174

Raine standing motionless in the middle of her room, staring at the door he had closed softly behind him.

In a departure from custom, Mary opened the door at Raine's knock instead of just calling "Come in" as she did usually. "Oh, Raine, I'm so glad you came first," Mary said with some agitation. "I wanted to talk to you before Nick gets here. I told him. I told him everything. He knows about Tony and my illness and how we met and . . . well, just everything!" She waved her hands rather wildly.

Raine responded neutrally, unwilling to admit that she knew and to admit *how* she came by her knowledge that Nick had been told everything by his mother. "How did Nick react, Mary?"

"He was shocked and upset," Mary said predictably. Raine agreed silently. She *knew* how upset Nick had been! "But he was wonderful," Mary continued. "He . . . he called me Mother. He hasn't done that since he . . . since that day. I think he's forgiven me or at least that he understands better now. It's going to be all right, Raine. For the first time in a long time, it's going to be all right."

Mary burst into tears. Raine soothed her, but didn't try to make her stop crying. These were healing tears, releasing accumulated tensions and washing away the fears Mary had harbored about Nick's reaction to what she had told him. Raine hoped that Nick would take a long time shaving because Mary needed this release.

When the flood had passed, Mary mopped her eyes and smiled. "Thank you, Raine. It doesn't embarrass you when I cry and that's rare. Emotion makes many people uncomfortable, I've noticed, but you treat it so naturally that I just sort of let myself go."

"Emotion *is* natural, Mary. Too often we suppress it when we shouldn't," Raine agreed. *But sometimes we have to suppress it when we don't want to,* she thought sadly to herself.

As if on cue, there came Nick's brief rap on the door. Mary squeaked and headed for the bedroom to repair her tear-drenched makeup. Raine went to let Nick in.

He was smiling warmly, a continuation of the smile he'd given her just before he'd left her room, but his dark eyes twinkled mischievously and warned her that he was prepared to be improper. "Good morning, Raine, darling," he said blithely, and she braced herself against a blush. "I hope you slept well last night. I—" his voice dropped teasingly "—had an excellent night."

Before she could say anything, his mood changed to one of serious inquiry and he said quietly, "How's Mary this morning?"

"She's all right now," Raine reassured him. "She cried, but it was good for her. Now she's repairing her makeup. Nick . . ." Raine hesitated and then finished. "Sometimes she'll need to cry. Let her. Hold her, comfort her, and that'll do her more good than the medicines in the long run."

"And when I need to cry, will you do the same for me?" he asked soberly.

Raine looked at him uncertainly, but before she could frame an answer, Mary came back and the moment was lost.

176

Breakfast was a rather subdued meal, but there was a warm camaraderie, almost a feeling of family that had been lacking before. Nick's mood could only be described as mellow and Mary radiated a quiet happiness, a serenity, which was touching. Raine looked from one to the other. Perhaps the price had not been too high after all.

They had just finished the last of their toast and were lingering over final cups of coffee when the phone rang. Nick was closest, so he lifted the receiver and listened briefly. A look of surprise flickered across his face but he responded, "Yes, she's here."

He didn't relinquish the phone to Mary. Instead he said curtly, "I'll give her the message," and dropped the receiver back into its rest.

The look he turned on Raine was enigmatic. "That was the desk. There's a man at reception. He wants to see you. He says his name is Fisher."

CHAPTER VIII

Raine sped across the lobby on winged feet and threw herself at the big blond man who stood with wide-open arms, braced to catch her. She flung her arms around his neck and hugged him with rapturous abandon, oblivious to onlookers, even to the one who had followed her across the lobby and now stood nearby, watching the reunion with a grim and scowling countenance.

Raine's first words did nothing to appreciably enlighten Nick's expression. "Jeff! Darling, darling Jeff! Where did you come from? Why are you here? How are the families? Is everyone well and is Megan with you?" She hugged him again and finished, "Oh, it's so *good* to see you!"

The blond man swung her off her feet, kissed her soundly, and responded with a beaming grin, "It's good to see you too, Raine, honey, and it's been too long since we *have* seen you! The families are fine and Megan's at home, which is where I've come from and where I want to take you." The man scanned her face carefully and said more quietly, "We've been worried about you, Raine. Mom and Aunt Beth got together and decided that you might like to see a friendly

179

family face. Megan volunteered mine. She said that it wasn't a particularly pretty one, but it was certainly friendly enough."

Raine laughed but tears glistened in her eyes. "It's a beautiful face, Jeff, and I'm very glad to see it. Mom and Aunt Beth were right. A family face is just what I do need to see right now."

By now Nick's expression had reached a new level of grimness. He stepped forward and said silkily, "I think it's time you introduced me, Raine." He held out a compelling hand to the man who had rested his large hands atop Raine's shoulders while they talked.

Raine started uncontrollably and whirled. She hadn't even known Nick was there. "Oh," she said faintly. Nick's expression was urbanely savage.

"I'm Nick Hunter," Nick announced, since Raine hadn't found her voice.

"I'm Jeff Fisher, Raine's brother-in-law," Jeff responded a trifle warily. He clasped Nick's hand firmly. His expression was clearly speculative when he looked from Nick down to the still speechless Raine.

"Have you registered yet?" Nick asked smoothly. "How long will you be visiting Raine?" Nick cast down the gauntlet with unmistakable emphasis.

Some indefinable tension eased within the larger man and he grinned faintly. "Oh, I imagine I'll stay just as long as Raine wants me to," he drawled as smoothly in his turn. "Her mother and my mother wouldn't have it any other way." He paused and added, "And neither would my wife, Megan, who is one of Raine's best and oldest friends."

Raine drew in a deep breath. There was no time

like the present. "Jeff will need a room just for to-night. *We'll* be leaving tomorrow morning." There, it had been said. She waited for Nick's reaction.

He didn't keep her waiting. "I'll have you shown to a room," Nick said smoothly to Jeff. "I'm sure you'll want to freshen up. Raine and I have something we must discuss." Nick reached out and slid his arm around Raine's shoulders, pulling her against his side. "We'll join you before lunch. I know my mother will be very happy to meet some of Raine's family."

Nick propelled Raine up to the reception desk with him, giving her no chance to take the coward's way out. There was no escape from Nick. She knew it was useless to try.

"Take Mr. Fisher's luggage to the green suite," Nick ordered briskly, and guided Raine toward his office with irresistible determination, not even allowing her a backward beseeching glance at Jeff.

He hustled her past the astounded Mrs. Bolt. Nick snarled out "No interruptions!" as he slammed the door shut behind them.

"Yes, sir!" Mrs. Bolt responded faintly to the blank panels of the door. "*Yesss,* sir!"

Nick directed Raine to the chair she had occupied once before and none too gently saw her seated in it. He then perched on the edge of his desk and loomed above her with an absolutely ferocious scowl narrowing his eyes and thinning the line of his mouth.

"It's time and past due for us to get a few things straight, Raine," Nick gritted out, "and the first one is that you're not going *anywhere* tomorrow with your brother-in-law."

"Oh, yes, I am, Nicholas Hunter!" Raine asserted roundly. "I am going home tomorrow. Your mother doesn't need me anymore, or at least," Raine amended with characteristic honesty, "she'll be able to get along without me now. She has you and you're what she's needed more than anything else. Your mother will understand."

"Damn it, woman! Are you trying to drive me insane? I'm not talking about my mother. I'm talking about me. You, me, we, us!" The intensity of his deep voice made his words carry more force than a shout.

"There is no us, Nick," Raine shot back stubbornly. "There's you and there is me and I am getting on a plane with Jeff tomorrow."

"There was an us last night," Nick said brutally.

Raine flushed hotly and her eyes dropped to her hands which were clenched in her lap. "I know," she admitted in a choked voice. Then, more strongly, she continued, "But that was last night. This is today."

Nick uttered a short expletive. "You can dismiss what happened between us so lightly?" he asked incredulously.

"No, not lightly." Raine almost cried. "But the . . . circumstances . . . were unusual. You needed someone." She wouldn't look up at him.

"Oh, no, Raine," Nick denied savagely. "I didn't need *someone*. I needed *you!* I came to *you* for comfort. And you're not some do-good volunteer, handing out doughnuts and coffee and cheer to the troops on their way to the front. You weren't just offering solace to someone who's been through the wars. That's not your style, lady. You'll give someone a helping hand, but not the rest of your body." His

182

words hammered away at her, trying to find a way through her tight defensive shell.

"Leave me alone, Nick," Raine begged. "What do you want of me? I can't give you what you want!" Tears gathered in the corners of her eyes.

"I want you to love me, Raine. I want you to admit that you love me."

The quiet sincerity of his deep voice jerked Raine's bent head up as though he'd yanked on a string connected to the top of her skull. Her eyes and her mouth rounded with shock.

Nick chopped out a sharp bark of laughter with no actual humor in it. "Took your breath away, did I? Well, there's more to come. I love you. I want to marry you."

It wasn't a tender declaration wrapped up with hearts and flowers, but Raine believed he meant what he said, at least the marriage part. He might want to marry her, but she doubted that love had anything to do with it.

Her obvious scepticism didn't surprise him. He rubbed the back of his neck with an almost weary gesture and smiled twistedly. "Not a graceful declaration, was it? I don't blame you for not placing too much credence in it, but I hadn't planned to make it quite so soon or in such circumstances, in the middle of a flaming argument! I wanted to ease you into the idea gently, to court you, if you'll forgive the rather archaic phrase."

"Oh, I believe your offer of marriage is sincere," Raine assured him with a sigh.

"But you don't believe I love you."

"No." Raine was blunt. "I know you want me, but that's not the same."

"No, it isn't the same," he agreed calmly. "I've wanted a number of women in my life. I've had enough experience to know the difference," he informed her coolly. He captured her blue eyes with his own dark ones. "I do know the difference, Raine. There weren't any of those women whom I wanted for more reason than the physical pleasure they could give me, and they all knew it. I didn't care about their minds or their feelings. I only required that their bodies please me."

Raine winced and Nick's face grew stern. "That was my life-style before I met you. I'm not going to apologize for it because it's in the past. You have your past as well. I'm not asking you to deny it. I don't want you to deny it. It's made you the woman I love." He half smiled. "In a way, Raine, you're more experienced than I am. You've loved, deeply and satisfyingly, and that's a part of your life that I can't match. I've never loved a woman before. I've never even used the words, in or out of bed. At least I wasn't a hypocrite about it, but that's about all that can be said for my former relationships."

Raine was listening intently now. This was a Nick she'd never suspected might exist, matured beyond her expectations and sharply self-aware as so few people are. She might come to *like* this Nick Hunter very much. But that was a far cry from loving and marrying him.

"Still not convinced?" Nick cut through her thoughts. "That's all right. I'm not finished yet. I didn't fall in love with you at first sight either, you know, and I think that last night you finally began to see me for the first time, so I won't ask for more than I was able to do myself. Take your time. We've got all day. We've got the rest of our lives, for that matter. I thought you were a lady on the make, out for what you could get," he continued. "I changed my opinion. You'll change yours about me."

"Nick, it's not just your . . . past." Raine phrased it delicately, entering the conversation at last. Nick had done the talking. It was time he did some listening. "Perhaps you are ready to make a commitment to a woman now—" she began.

"Call it by the right name," he interrupted her harshly. "Call it love. And not *a* woman. You. Only you. For the rest of my life."

She didn't comment directly, but her voice, when she continued, was low and slightly desperate. He was knocking down her straw men one by one. "You're grateful for what I did for Mary. I don't accept that gratitude is a proper foundation for marriage."

He snorted. "Don't be an idiot! I am grateful for what you've done for my mother and I love you because of it," he said crisply, "but I wouldn't *marry* you for that feeble kind of reason, and you know it. I love you because you're the type of person who *could* do what you have done, not because you've *done* it. There is a difference and we both know it." His voice took on a tinge of irritation as he said, "Nor do I want to marry you to make my mother's last days happy," thus ruthlessly disposing of another point he was sure she'd been prepared to raise.

"I like to travel," Raine stated in an argumentative

185

voice, as though he might be prepared to chain her hand and foot to the nearest slot machine.

"We'll travel," he said briefly. "Not right away, of course. There's Mary to consider, but afterward—" his voice broke slightly "—I can be free for fairly long stretches of time. We'll both have to make adjustments to our life-styles, Raine. That's part of marriage."

Nick was smashing through Raine's flimsy barricades faster than she could put them together and she was feeling hounded and driven. Nick stalked her from one shelter to another, inexorably flushing her from the thicket of each evasion, forcing her nearer and nearer to the truth he was determined to make her face.

"Run out of excuses, Raine?" Nick asked dryly when she'd sat silently for a long moment. "Why don't you try the last one? Tell me that you don't love me."

"I . . ." Her voice stayed in her throat, but she cleared it and began again bravely. "I don't love you, Nick," she half whispered.

"At last," he growled on a strange, exultant note. He stood up, yanked her from her chair and kissed her. She struggled briefly, but it was a short and unequal battle.

By the time the kiss ended, Raine's arms were looped tightly around Nick's neck and her traitorous body had admitted what her mind would not. If Nick wanted her, he could have her and there didn't seem to be anything she could do about it.

He lifted his mouth from hers, no more than a

whisper away, and said softly, *"Now* say it, little liar. Tell me you don't love me."

"It's not love," Raine whispered brokenly, but she didn't struggle to be free. She'd never be free of him again.

"It *is* love!" he contradicted her fiercely. "You love me. Admit it, Raine. Admit it!"

"I want you," she moaned, twisting her body against his. "I want you."

"That's not enough." Nick wouldn't accept the half a loaf she offered him. "I want it all, everything you have to give. It's still there, Raine, all the warmth, all the commitment. Give it to *me,"* he urged her. "I'm not Johnny. I'll never ask you for what was his. I want what is *mine."* The demand in his voice was implacable. He gave no quarter.

Somewhere deep within, an unacknowledged barrier crumbled. The final frozen knot of residual anguish melted away in a healing stream of hot tears. Nick scooped her up into his arms and carried her over to a small couch. He sank down, still cradling her tightly against his chest and held her while she wept away a grief which was years old.

When she finally hiccupped to a shuddering calm, he mopped her face with a clean white handkerchief and then held it while she blew a sniffly nose. She curled against his body and tucked her face into his warm neck, much as a kitten might snuggle into trusted arms. He didn't speak. He'd said what he had to. The next words must come from her.

Raine felt drained, and yet curiously renewed. She was empty, but she knew that with a word, a sentence, she would be filled, fulfilled.

"I love you, Nick."

It was a breath, a mere whisper of words, but he heard. It was so easy to say now, that small sentence that had cost so much, but which was worth every tear of the price. Nick sagged back against the couch, the relaxation of his hard body poignantly expressive of relief. She felt his chest rise and fall in a deep breath and she knew, without words, that he'd paid too, that her pain had been his as well. He did love her.

He understood her too—better, in many ways, than she'd understood herself. He had known that the language of her body had spoken far more truthfully than the words from her mouth. When she had accepted . . . *No, be honest, Raine,* she chided herself silently. When she had *welcomed* him to her bed, she had committed herself to him. If she had not loved him then, she would have sent him away to find surcease elsewhere—in the depths of a bottle or in another woman's arms.

It was ironic in a way, that Nick, who had lived all his adult life without ever making the commitment of love, should be the one to recognize it so surely when it burgeoned between them. She, who had lived all her life surrounded by love, had fled from it, refusing to allow herself to recognize, to admit to love, because it might not be matched in depth or duration. She had refused to trust either Nick or her instincts and, cowardlike, had been prepared to demean what had passed between them.

She would have, but Nick wouldn't let her. His love had been strong enough for both of them.

"You'd like to be married from your parents'

home, wouldn't you?" Nick's deep voice cut through her silent soliloquy. "Will Johnny's parents mind?"

Raine felt a welling upsurge of love for Nick. He understood her so thoroughly, his instinct of love leading him where she would not have thought he could go. "No, they won't mind. They'll be happy for us both. My Aunt Beth and my Uncle Jason are very special people. You'll love them and they'll love you, I promise." Raine chuckled, a blue devil of mischief dancing in her eyes. "You're about to be inundated in family, my darling."

"Say that again," he said huskily, his hands roving lightly but surely over her pliant body.

"What? About family?" Raine's voice was puzzled and a little breathless.

"No," Nick mumbled into the soft skin of her neck. "Call me your darling. Call my name again."

Raine turned into his demanding embrace, lifting her face for his kiss. There would be time later for other things. Soon they would go to tell Mary and Jeff. With Mary and Jeff they would travel home, where she would take Nick's ring upon her finger and take his name as her own, visible symbols of the invisible but nonetheless tangible reality of their pledge to each other. But for now, she called his name. His name was love.

LOOK FOR NEXT MONTH'S
CANDLELIGHT ECSTASY ROMANCES™: